MW01717541

SEX A BALLER!

Out Of His

Mind & Money!

By Mysterious Luva

SEX A BALLER

By Mysterious Luva Is Published By:

BLACK PEARL BOOKS

P.O. Box 361985 • Decatur, Georgia 30036-1985 • 404-735-3553

All Black Pearl Books titles, imprints and distributed lines are available at special quantity discounts for bulk purchases for sales promotion, premiums, fund raising, educational or institutional use.

Special book excerpts or customized printings can also be created to fit specific needs. For details, write to Black Pearl Books: Attention Senior Publisher, P.O. Box 361985, Decatur, Georgia 30036-1985 or visit website: www.BlackPearlBooks.com

BOOKSTORE DISTRIBUTION

Contact: Black Pearl Books Inc.
P.O. Box 361985
Decatur, Georgia 30036-1985
1-404-735-3553

ISBN: 0-9728005-1-4

First Trade Paperback Printing: January 2004

Cover Credits

Design: Marion Designs (www.mariondesigns.com)

Special Note: *The person appearing on the cover of this book is a model and NOT Mysterious Luva!*

Printed in the United States of America

Introduction

So, You Say You Want A Baller, Huh?

Most women say that to themselves, but aren't committed to the game. I'm talkin' real dedication to the craft. That's what it takes to identify, get and keep a real baller!

Catchin' a baller is a full-time job. There ain't no vacation days or holidays. You've got to be ready at all times, have your eyes open and know what the hell you're doing!

There's no room for weakness or shame in your game, or you'll be the one getting played. There can be no limit to the length you'll go or you'll lose your golden goose to some other woman that's taking this shit seriously.

If you think you can get a baller simply because you think that you're fine, you're already lost. While good looks are a step in the right direction, there's much more to this quest than just that.

If you think you got the ill na-na, poo-tain, kitty, pussy or whatever you call it and that a man can't resist you after you *put it on him*—you're lost too. I'll be the first to admit, turnin' a baller out in bed is a nice bonus, but that don't mean you can get that nigga's money. And that's what this game is all about.

Understanding a baller from the inside and out is what will make you successful in catching ballers.

This book will take you through an interesting journey of becoming a superb baller-catcher. I'll also share tips & secrets to help make your baller-catching efforts more successful. But, you've gotta be willing to learn!

SEX A BALLER!

Out Of His

Mind & Money!

By Mysterious Luva

Chapter One My Sexual Beginning

I've always loved dick. I wouldn't even attempt to lie about it. The way a lubricated rock-hard dick feels in my hands just before it's about to cum, or the way a nice-size dick feels hitting the walls inside of me just right .....ummphhh ..... there ain't nothing like it! However, I've learned that there is only one thing that beats out a nice dick ... money!

My love of the dick began with my first sexual encounter at the very young age of just thirteen. Unknown to my mother, a devout Christian woman, I was secretly dating a 17-year old star football player named Andrè that I'd met one Saturday in a local mall near my hometown of Lithonia, Georgia, a suburb of Atlanta.

Though my face and hair looked every bit of thirteen, my body had blossomed early to that of a 19-year old's. And, I was getting regular attention from much older boys and even some men 18 and over.

I had to be careful so that my mother wouldn't find out that I was dating Andrè. I knew that she wouldn't approve. First of all, because I wasn't allowed to date at all, not even a boy that was my age. And certainly not one that was four years older than me.

My mother did her best to make it difficult for me to have opportunities to see boys. But, because she was a single parent that had to work and money was very tight, at age thirteen, I spent my first summer at home alone. Sure, my mother would call home about every two hours to check on me or have a retired deaconess from our church occasionally stop by unexpectedly. My mother even used all of her vacation and sick days during that summer-break to reduce the number of days I'd be home by myself. But, for most of the days, I was still on my own until she got home around 5 pm.

Mysterious Luva

Normally, I spent much of my day talking to Andrè on the phone after my mother had gone to work. The only times I got off the phone with him was when my mother was most-likely gonna call to check on me. I knew when her break-times were, so I was careful to already be off the phone 'cause I knew she'd be able to tell that I had clicked-over and she'd be asking who I was on the phone with.

On a very special Wednesday, Andrè called me early in the morning and asked if he could come over. I hesitated because I knew that if I got caught having a boy over the house that there would be hell to pay. At the same time, I didn't want Andrè to think of me as young and unable to make my own decisions, so I said yes.

I was nervous about being alone with Andrè, so I called my girlfriend Sherry to see if she would come over too. She was there at the mall when I first met Andrè.

"Hello", Sherry answered.

"Sherry, Andrè asked if he could come over. I told him okay, but I'm kinda scared. Can you come over right now?", I ramble with urgency.

I could tell something was different in Sherry's voice. She couldn't speak freely because her mother was home preparing to take her to an orthodontist appointment.

"Yeah girl, that top and pants go together", Sherry spoke in code to avoid detection by her mother of the details of our conversation. "Go ahead and wear that, I'll call you when I get back from the orthodontist", Sherry said convincingly, as I could hear her mother beckoning for her to get off the phone because they were already late for the appointment.

Though Sherry couldn't be my safety-blanket, I took her coded comments to mean that I shouldn't worry or be nervous.

The house was already clean, my mother made sure that I kept everything in order, so I spent most of the 20-minutes it took Andrè to get to my house combing and re-combing my permed shoulder-length hair trying to get it to look just right.

When I heard a knock on the back door, my heart began racing. At the same time, I felt a sense of relief that Andrè had sense enough to park in the alley around the back of my house instead of in the front, because I was sure my mom had a neighborhood spy.

SEX A BALLER

As I opened the door, I was greeted with an ear-to-ear smile of my handsome 6'2 Andrè. His smile was so contagious I had to fold my lips in to keep from looking like he was the first guy that'd ever been to my house.

After I'd finished locking the back door and turned around, Andrè was standing there with his arms open.

"Can a brother get a hug?", he said smoothly and authoritatively.

I re-folded my lips in again as I stepped inside his awaiting arms. He hugged and held me tightly within his muscular arms as my chest pressed against his rippled body. His hands caressed up and down my back as he swayed me from side-to-side. I would've stayed in his arms longer, but his firm embrace was creating an embarrassing tingle in my breasts as I felt my nipples beginning to harden. So, I broke free of what was supposed to be a simple greeting hug that had already lasted 15-seconds too long. I made my escape in the name of house-guest-courtesy by walking into the kitchen and offering him something to drink.

When I returned to the living room with a tall glass of orange punch, Andrè had already made himself comfortable on the sofa, remote in hand, flipping through cable channels like it was a video photo album.

"Here you go", I said placing his drink in front of him and uncomfortable as to where I should sit.

As I began making my way to a love seat adjacent to the main sofa Andrè was sitting on, he waved me over.

"Why you goin' sit way over there? I came all the way over to see you and you're not gonna even sit by me?", Andrè said before gulping down half of his drink.

I obliged by sitting down next to him, as my eyes peeked at the clock above the television. It read 10:15 am. I wanted to keep track of the time because I knew my mom would be calling on her lunch break between noon and 12:45 pm.

Andrè wrapped his right arm around me. My head instinctively rested on his chest/shoulder area and my hand on his toned stomach muscles. We stayed in that cuddled position, as I was enjoying the smell of his masculine cologne and the gliding of his hand on the side of my waist and back. Abruptly, he then leaned backward. As I looked up to see what was wrong, Andrè planted my first-ever kiss from a boy on my lips, which quickly turned into my first-ever French-kiss. As our tongues swirled and his hand swirling moved from my waist to my butt, I felt a butterfly feeling in my stomach shortly before my juices began flowing between my legs.

Without delay, Andrè removed his hand from my butt and slid it underneath my shirt and grabbed a firm hold onto my right breast, rubbing and squeezing it. When he lifted up my bra, my nipple was hard enough to dial a phone number on a rotary phone. His large fingers traveling atop of my stretched-out nipple was a feeling of pleasure and slight stingy-ness. My eyes were squinted closed, my lips pressed together while Andrè kissed my neck. The seal of my lips was broken when he began to pinch my nipple between two of his fingers. It marked the first time I'd heard the melodious sound of my own groaning as my eyes rolled inside my shut eyelids and I attempted to endure.

Andrè moved my hands to his pants and I felt the outline of his penis bulging through his jeans. It was bigger, longer and harder than I was expecting a guy's penis to feel.

As Andrè re-positioned himself, pulled my shirt completely off over my head and slid my bra away, nervousness overwhelmed me. There I was, topless and fully-exposed. Nipples standing out like fingers pointing. My eyes didn't know where to look, so I found myself looking down and off to the side instead of making direct eye-contact with Andrè, just in case my body was disappointing to him.

Andrè knelt between my legs and gripped both of my C-cup breasts, one in each hand, pinching both nipples with equal strength, as my mouth opened wide and my head whipped back against the head-rest of the sofa. As he slid his body upward, pressing the hardening dick in his jeans between my legs, he began sucking my nipples and my body began to shiver. My wide-open mouth had closed a bit to a rounded O-shape and I was exhaling more frequently in heavy bursts of air. Each burst of air that exited my mouth was strong enough to blow out all the candles on my last birthday cake.

Then Andrè removed his shirt, un-did his belt-buckle, button and unzipped his pants, before again sitting next to my still heavily breathing body on the sofa. His arm pulled me into the warm cuddle of earlier, except this time our naked upper-torso flesh was making sensual contact. With his left hand he unbuttoned and unzipped my jeans, before taking my hand and placing it inside of his pants. The inaugural feel of a dick in my hand was somewhat eerie. Though it was hard, it did feel a little rubbery.

Once my hand was solidly wrapped around his dick, Andrè slid his pants completely off onto the floor, allowing me to get my first clear view of a dick. I couldn't help but stare at it, as it was proudly standing tall. My eyes scanned it like it was the last time I'd see one.

As I continued admiring it's shape and size, especially the way the circumcised head looked peering above the top of my gripping hand, I then began to feel the forceful throbbing of it in my hand and immediately gained respect for its power and for what it could do to me.

After Andrè had taught my hand how to stroke his dick until it had increased to an even greater size, it was apparently my turn to show him what I had, as he slid my hips out of my jeans. Still embarrassed about my body, I closed my legs immediately after my jeans fell next to his on the floor. That is, until Andrè used his arm like a crowbar and his speech like United Nations Negotiator by whispering assurances in my ear that everything was okay.

With the very first touch of his hand across my pussy, my thighs commenced to shaking feverishly, my head jerked and my mouth grunted a series of redundant *ohhhs*. My legs kept trying to clamp closed. At one point, Andrè had to slide one of his legs over mine to keep them open. When his fingers paid special attention to my clit, my entire body got tense and convulsed in seizure-style. All thoughts were foggy until he penetrated me with his finger. I didn't know it then, but the in-and-out friction motion of his finger created my first orgasm.

As Andrè prepared himself to penetrate me with his dick, I was not only scared about it hurting, but also about getting pregnant.

"Wait. I don't wanna get pregnant!", I cautioned to Andrè.

"You won't. I promise.", Andrè assured me as he was raising my legs.

"Oww, oww, oww", I cried out as he entered me.

André's dick was so large as compared to his finger and it hurt for the initial 4-minutes. As my pussy began to relax, pain gave way to enormous pleasure as I began to think, *No wonder why mom didn't want me to experience sex – It feels so good!*

André proceeded to fuck the shit out of me that morning. The alternating speed of his pumping had me cumming more times than I could count. And as promised, André pulled out before climaxing, spewing his white milky substance on my tummy.

After André left, I spent the early part of the afternoon eliminating any evidence of his visit. Cleared the air of its sex-scent with Lysol spray and washed the cup he drank from and placed it back in the cabinet. The remainder of the afternoon I used for daydreaming and reminiscing about my first sexual encounter. I didn't even share what I'd done with my girlfriend Sherry because I knew she had a big mouth. And, I didn't want the news to get around and make its way up to someone's parent who'd call my mother.

I never would've predicted how much that one day would change my life. I'd discovered my womanhood. I'd unleashed my desires and was all the more anxious to do it again and again.

While lying in bed, late at night, I'd found that by playing with myself, I possessed the power to make myself orgasm. And so I did this…often.

André and I fucked many more times over the next year until he left for college on a football scholarship. It was hard for me because my *first* was away at school and I couldn't even call him because my mother would know that we'd had a relationship.

I wrote him letters, but told him not to write back because my mom normally checked the mail before I could.

It was shear agony waiting for him to come back home during his college holiday breaks. I longed for him each and everyday. I was living a one-sided love affair.

Over the Christmas break, we got together for the first time in what felt like years. But things seemed to have changed. He acted different. And wasn't as excited as he'd been before about me. It was as though he'd out-grown me. It hurt me real bad.

Though we did have sex over the school-break, that too felt differently. Andrè was doing it more out of opportunity than genuine affection. I couldn't figure out what I was doing wrong or why things had changed.

After his freshman year in college, we never had sex again, as he was now dating college girls and I was just a sophomore in high school. But all in all, I was grateful to him for having been my first.

»»»»»»»»»»»»»»»«««««««««««««««

By the time I was a senior in high school, my freaky-side had fully bloomed.

Though just 17-years old, I had the sexual resumè of a 30-year old women. I'd sucked dick, had oral performed on me, done anal with a finger, used a dildo and even French-kissed with my girl, Sherry. Not to mention that I'd slept with nearly 20 different men, the oldest being Mr. Peterson, a 42-year old history teacher at my school whose class I was failing. That is, until I fucked my way to a B+. I think I could've gotten an A+ from him if I'da let him fuck my ass like he wanted to do. But a B+ was good enough to keep my mom from going nuts over my grades.

It was after sex with the history teacher that I was awakened to what I could get by using my body. A lesson that would take me far in the future.

Chapter Two Buck Wild

Throughout my high school years, my mother and I battled often over the types of guys I was dating. Mom wanted me to date young men from the church, but I preferred guys with an edgier side. Further complicating our relationships was the discovery of a paycheck stub during spring cleaning of the attic in our home.

My mother, who was very much into the church, so much so she was considering going into the ministry had a dark past that she'd hidden from me. Beginning when I was just three years old, at the time my father abandoned us, my mother made ends meet by dancing at an exotic strip club.

So, who is she to criticize my behavior?, I thought to myself.

That discovery altered our communications, at the time it was most crucial to me.

After graduation, despite being smart enough to attend college, I decided against doing so because it would mean getting financial assistance from my mother, which I wasn't going to do. Instead, I moved into an apartment in the Decatur area of Atlanta, paid for by Mr. Peterson. Originally, Mr. Peterson had declined to pay for it but later changed his mind when I reminded him that I was under-18 when we'd first had sex.

Mr. Peterson was married. And, as a high school teacher, he wasn't rolling in dough. As a cover-story to his wife, Mr. Peterson worked summer school and claimed to donate his summer salary back to the school district to help with budgetary crunches. I couldn't believe how stupid Mrs. Peterson must've been.

Through my ability to get my living expenses paid for by Mr. Peterson, I was learning more than I'd ever learned at Redan High School.

The threat of revealing Mr. Peterson's under-age sex act with me was more powerful than actually exposing it. With the threat, I could control him over and over again. And I did. My first car was purchased at an auction by him.

Though I didn't have to, I continued having sex with Mr. Peterson. And it had nothing to do with him paying for the apartment or buying my first car. He was a handsome, sexy black man. About 6'3, athletic build, dark-skinned with naturally wavy hair. What kept me glued to him sexually was that he had a man's dick and knew how to use it. Mr. Peterson fucked me better than anyone I'd had sex with before. And he was unexpectedly freaky for what one would think of a history teacher.

Mr. Peterson would bring over sex toys – dildos and other battery-operated gadgets. He enjoyed watching me make myself cum. I enjoyed it too. Whenever I knew that he was coming over, I'd be filled with anticipation of what new sex act I was going to experience. I had turned into the horniest of freaks. But, unlike my mother I was determined not to be ashamed of it or hide it.

Sherry, my girlfriend since way back in junior high school, was attending Georgia Perimeter College. The campus was near my apartment, so it was almost like having a roommate, 'cause she was over so much. I didn't mind though. We had a lot in common. Both of us didn't know our fathers, battled with our mothers and were outwardly candid about our freaky sexuality.

I'd known Sherry was bisexual since she was a junior in high school. One thing she could not stand was being labeled as a lesbian! She liked both men and women.

Though we had much in common, we were very different physically. Sherry was a deep brown-skinned brickhouse, with shoulder-length hair. Though we both weighed the same, about 135-pounds, at just 5'3, Sherry had curves that made her reminiscent of a thicker-Lil' Kim, except her D-cup breasts were real. And if you looked up the word Bootylicious in the dictionary, you'd certainly see Sherry's picture right next to Beyoncè. I, on the other hand, was a little leaner because of my 5'6" height. But, I must say, I had some decent curves, myself. My breasts were a very-respectable C-cup, legs like Ashanti and nice booty too. It just was tougher to appreciate my body while standing next to a girl who's booty stuck out like she had a basketball stuffed in the back of her jeans.

During one afternoon in November, Sherry came over to my apartment to hang-out as we often did. She was out of school because of the Thanksgiving break. We were drinking strawberry daiquiris and thumbing through our high school year book, laughing at geeky pictures of people we knew.

When we came upon a picture of Mr. Peterson, I quickly turned the page. I didn't keep too much from Sherry, except for things that I really, really didn't want to get out, like me having sex with Mr. Peterson.

Sherry insisted that I turn back to the page.

"Do you remember Mr. Peterson's boring class?", Sherry said with a tipsy smile.

"Yeah.", blandly I responded, as I turned away from the page once again.

Out of nowhere Sherry began laughing to herself like she was watching a bad act on *Showtime At The Apollo*.

"Gurrll, what's wrong with you?", I giggled at her giggling. "Are you drunk already?"

"No, no, I just thought of something funny, that's all", she said as laughter resumed in her.

"What's so funny?", I questioned.

"Well, it ain't really funny…it's…just…nevermind", Sherry said attempting to abort.

"Oh no you're not gonna leave me hangin'! What is it?", I pressed.

"Okay, I guess it's alright to tell you now. But I still want you to promise that this stays between me and you", Sherry insisted.

"Okay, damn girl, whatever, what is it?", I said tired of her stalling.

"Back in high school, I fucked Mr. Peterson to get a better grade on a mid-term exam that I flunked", Sherry revealed.

I actually was stunned by the news. Even a little disappointed. Apparently Mr. Peterson was making it a practice to sleep with underachieving female students. Up to this point, what Mr. Peterson and I had done seemed special. But I guess I was just one of many.

The disappointments were starting to pile up. First learning that my own mother was a stripper and now hearing about Mr. Peterson. I was busy reflecting on my disappointments, I didn't even hear Sherry talking to me.

"....Mysterious, Mysterious...Did you hear what I said?", Sherry questioned, confused as to why I hadn't responded with a comment to such a bomb she'd just dropped.

I snapped out my daze. Then, my disappointment in Mr. Peterson turned to a *fuckit* attitude.

"Yeah, I heard you. You know what? I fucked Mr. Peterson, too", proudly I said.

"You did?", Sherry was as shocked to hear about me as I was about her.

"Hell, yeah!", I aggressively charged.

At the time I didn't care whether Sherry would tell people or not. After getting over my feelings of hurt, I realized that she would not because she had sex with him too.

There was a slight pause in the room as neither one of us knew what to say next.

"Well, um, he sure gives some good dick!", Sherry broke the awkward silence with her humorous declaration that drew a smile of agreement from me.

"True dat", I said giving her a ghetto-fab high-five.

We continued making daiquiris until we'd drank ourselves into a more sedated state. At which time, we mapped out a plan of surprise for good 'ol Mr. Peterson. Once we'd put the finishing touches on the plan, Sherry was ready to leave, but I thought that she was too drunk to drive.

"Sherry you can stay here tonight or at least let me call you a cab', I tried to convince her with options.

"Naw, I'm alright", she slurred as she couldn't find her car keys that were two feet away from her on the end table next to the sofa. "Damn, where are my keys?", she said as she wobbled a bit as she slow spun around glancing possible location in my apartment.

I was determined to not let her drive in her present condition, so I didn't aid her in finding the keys. I figured that I'd be able to talk some sense into her while she was busy searching. Unfortunately, she'd found the keys before I had a chance.

"Sherry, I can't let you drive like this", I urged.

"Girl, quit being so dramatic. I'll admit I'm buzzin' a little bit, but I can drive. I'll call you when I get home", Sherry said attempting to make her way to the front door.

I rushed past her and blocked her exit, throwing body in front of the door.

"Mysterious. Why you trippin'?", Sherry said with attitude that resembled sobriety, causing me to question whether or not I was trippin'.

Choosing to err on the side of caution, solidly I remained as a human barricade at my front door.

"Okay, I'm serious, let me go", Sherry demanded while she tried to reach the door handle.

"I'm serious too", I stood firm, countering whatever move she tried.

Finally, it semi-appeared that she'd given up, but I wasn't certain, as it appeared that she was going to make one last attempt by pulling me off the door. To my surprise, her final attempt was not to get through me, but to me, as she stepped right up to me and started gently kissing me on the neck. I thought it may have been a trick to get me to drop my arms down, allowing her to make her escape. So, I didn't drop my arms. Instead, I tried to nudge her away with my shoulders. When she dropped her purse to the floor and grabbed hold of both of my breasts, I knew for sure, leaving the apartment wasn't foremost on her mind anymore.

I was not gay or lesbian, but I was somewhat attracted to women. Meaning, I recognized a cute women when I saw one and not that I was sexually attracted by sight.

Sherry and I had shared a dare-game kiss back in high school, but nothing more. Her hands caressing and squeezing my breasts seemed awkward, but still I'd hesitated to stop it and found my hands went from blocking the door to resting on her shoulders instead of pulling her hands off my tits. I questioned myself as to the reason for my delay, at the same time I was enjoying her nipple-hardening caresses.

"Sherry, c'mon now…stop playing", I said finally, wrapping my hands around her wrists attempting to release her grip on my breasts.

"What, Mysterious?", Sherry questioned staring me straight in the eye, but not yet releasing my breasts from her grip.

I looked away because I didn't know what to say. I didn't want to hurt her by rejection. I just kinda wished it wasn't happening, but I would be lying if I said it wasn't feeling good.

"I'on know….I'm just….You know I….", I stumbled-out an attempt to communicate what wasn't even clear to me.

"This don't make you gay, or lesbian, Mysterious", Sherry said in a tone that was like she was almost disappointed that she had to even say those words.

"It's not that…I…mmphh", I stammered, frustrated by my lack of being able to define my awkward feelings.

Using my moment of hesitation, Sherry lifted my shirt and bra all in one motion and had her mouth around my nipples before I could decide to tell her to stop. Her tongue's swirling had me gritting my teeth and my panties wet. The size of her hands was smaller than what I was used to having grip my breast, but my nipples were every bit just as hard as any man-hands could create.

Convinced that she'd gotten me pass my reservations-state, Sherry French-kissed me before removing my shirt and guiding me by the hand to my sofa. *The best kiss I've ever had is by a woman?*, I remember thinking on the way to the sofa. My hands were actually shaking as we sat down. I hadn't been this nervous since my first-time with Andrè.

Sherry straddled me, pulled her shirt over her head, unsnapped her bra and cupped her breasts in her own hands while leaning forward towards my mouth. I'd never had this close of a view of another woman's breasts for as I long as I was having right then. Sherry's were beautiful, with narrow long nipples that I watched growing right in front of me.

Finally, I gave in to any residual reservations I was subconsciously harboring and began to suck on her tits. It wasn't gross or like anything I'd expected to feel. Actually, I loved the feeling of her nipples rubbing against my tongue. Soon, I had both of my hands squeezing the shit out of her big-ass titties and biting her nipples until she was moaning her satisfaction. I did my best to immolate what guys had done to me.

Just as I was getting very comfortable with tittie-sucking, Sherry stepped the game up. She unbuttoned my jeans and slid me out of them. Then encourage me to do the same to her. As she sat down next to me, Sherry grabbed my hand and guided it to rubbing across her wet pussy. That feel did take a moment for the awkwardness to wane. Sherry's extreme arousal and subsequent orgasmic gyrations aided me to concentrate more on trying to make her cum, than about how weird it felt to be touching her pussy.

"Ohhh, Mysteeer…Ree….uss", Sherry groaned near climax.

Just as everything before it had been, hearing my name used in a female-pitched passion-filled grunt was a very strange sound.

As I continued to rub my fingers back-n-forth across her pussy, faster and faster, her butt raised completely off the sofa and she struggled to look at me before her whole body erupted in a convulsing mode I'd never witnessed before…. with a woman, that is.

"Ahhhh, shit, ahhh, shit, I'm cumming! I'm cumming!", Sherry exclaimed as she forced my hand to continue it's fast-paced stroking until she'd released a full-orgasm. I was trippin' watching my girl in that position and completely out-of-control. And to think that it was my hand that created her to this state was mind-boggling.

It took several minutes for to her fully recover. Occasionally her head would jerk forward from some residual stimulation. It wasn't until her face changed from a serious-look to an ear-grinning smile that I knew that she was revitalized.

Sherry began with me by kneeling between my legs. Then she raised and opened them using her hands on my thighs. Using her thumb and a forefinger on her left hand she reached around my thigh spread my pussy open, licked two fingers on her right hand and began brushing my clit with them. I couldn't believe how quickly I was losing control, faster than I had with any man. Less than 45-seconds of this treatment had my stomach contracting the way it normally did before I orgasmed.

"Oh shit, Sherry!", I cried out before my eyes rolled so far into the top of my head that it hurt.

Undeterred, Sherry continued finger-massaging me until my body turned into shaking *Jello* and I could feel the cream flowing out of me. As if that weren't enough, she persisted by sucking and tongue-flicking my clit while inserting both fingers in me. Sherry's instincts and experience was incredible. It was the fastest and most efficient orgasm that I'd ever had created. A steady, rapid climb to ecstasy with no delay. Every touch useful and created ultimate stimulation. When I finally escaped the orgasm-hold that Sherry had on me by literally pulling her hands off of me, I couldn't deny the benefits of sex with a woman. And now I understood why Sherry also liked being with women. A woman understands the female body and can better give the attention a woman desires. Mentally understanding the benefits, however did nothing to reduce my love of a man's dick.

After we'd finished driving each other wild, Sherry and I took separate showers and didn't even talk about what just had happened. Sherry wasn't looking for me to be her girlfriend, she knew better. I think she was satisfied that I'd unchained myself by trying something new.

Chapter Three Taste Of The Bling

Two weeks after Sherry and I had *gotten busy*, we had exercised our plan on Mr. Peterson. I'd invited Mr. Peterson to my apartment. Shock was the look on his face when he arrived and saw Sherry also sitting there.

We cleared the air about each of our under-age sexual relationships purely for the purpose of watching him squirm. Neither one of us had any intentions of pursuing the matter in any other manner. Though it was not our original intent, we left that meeting with $3,000 in Mr. Peterson's hush-money that we'd later split.

Sherry and I were so amazed by what we could get from Mr. Peterson that we vowed to use every man for what they had. We figured men had been doing it to women for years, and what was wrong with flipping the table.

We had future plans to extort more money from Mr. Peterson, but four days after receiving the hush-money, he died from a stress-related heart attack.

I felt a little bad because I'd wondered if part of the stress was caused by our financial demands on him. However, I didn't have time to wallow in pity because I quickly had to find a way to pay the bills that Mr. Peterson had been paying.

I needed money quick and didn't know where I was gonna get it from. I know it sounds unsympathetic, but it was a good thing that I had $1500, my share of the hush-money from Mr. Peterson to tie me over.

Further complicating the matter for me was that between the time we got the hush money and the day he died, Mr. Peterson had come to my apartment and confided a long-kept secret. He was Sherry's father. Sherry's mother and Mr. Peterson had vowed to keep that fact a secret because Mr. Peterson was married at the time they had sex.

That's one of the reasons I only felt a little bad about his death. What I was doing by extorting Mr. Peterson wasn't exactly right, but nowhere near as wrong as what he'd done -- fucked his own daughter. And, he knew that she was his daughter when he did it.

The person I really felt bad for was Sherry. She had no idea and I wasn't gonna be the one to tell her. I knew that she always wanted to know who her father was and argued with her mother because she wouldn't tell her.

Even though I'd lost a lot of respect for Sherry's mom too, by learning about who Sherry's dad was, I briefly considered talking to her about it. I was worried that she might decide tell Sherry who her father was now that Mr. Peterson was dead, all the while unaware that that bastard had slept with Sherry. But, I just didn't.

» » » » » » » » » » » » » » » » » « « « « « « « « « « « « « « « «

I went by several strip-clubs looking to earn some quick cash. Even auditioned at a couple. But, when I came back in the evening to get a feel for where I'd be working, I didn't like it. The parking lots didn't feel safe, nor did the atmosphere inside feel right. Plus, I had no idea how much I'd have to invest just to start as a stripper. I'd have to buy costumes, a permit to dance, and new shoes because the clubs had a policy that dancers must wear high-heels and I had none. Shit! I was looking to make quick money not spend it.

On my way out of one of the clubs, disappointed because I still hadn't solved how I was gonna be paying rent or bills, I grabbed one of the complimentary sex magazines from the rack. At home, thumbing through it, I came across an ad that was looking for women escorts. The name of the company was Elite Escorts and the ad said that I could make $500 to $1,000 in one night.

The next morning I called Sherry to tell her about the ad and suggested that she come with me. She was *down*. I knew she would be.

Both Sherry and I were trippin' when we drove up to the luxury office building in the city of Alpharetta and saw how nice it actually looked. It was a large building with a security desk and everything. I guess we assumed it would be trashy-looking. I mean, we weren't stupid. We had a pretty good idea of the type of work we'd be doing to get $500 to $1,000 a night.

As we walked past people in business suits on our way to the security counter to sign-in, both of us felt a little out of place and definitely under-dressed in our hoochie-tight jeans and belly-out tops.

Even the security guard knew where we were going before we said a single word.

"Are you looking for Elite Escorts?", he said standing up so that he could scan his eyes over our young frames.

"Umm-hmm", we said quickly, almost ashamed that he'd asked so loudly.

"Take the elevators to the 11th floor, turn right, it's suite 1134", he said pointing in the direction of the elevators.

I was in a hurry to get out of the lobby, as I felt uncomfortable like everyone was looking at us. As we were about to turn the corner I glanced back at the security desk and the officer was still standing with his eyes glued to the back of Sherry's jeans. It made me wish that we could change clothes that instant.

When we made it to the Elite Escorts office, it looked just like any other business suite. A receptionist desk, waiting area and a coffee table with magazines on it.

"Hello, welcome to Elite Escorts, how may I help you?", the bubbly receptionist greeted us without assumption, better than the security guard had.

"Hi, my name is Mysterious Luva and she's Sherry Hughes. We have an appointment with Jim Koen", I spoke confidently.

"Okay, you can have a seat while I let him know that you're hear.", the receptionist smiled back to us, as she picked up the phone to call him.

We didn't have to wait long, as a surprisingly young white man, I'd say about 28 or so, came around the corner.

"Mysterious and Sherry?", he said.

"Yes.", we responded in unison like the *Double-Mint* twins.

"Come on back.", he motioned us with his arm.

We followed him to his spacious corner office and sat in the two leather chairs in front of his desk.

"What can I do for you guys today?", Jim surprised me by saying. I just assumed he'd be giving us the run-down.

Sherry and I looked at each other like we were trying to figure out who had the brain.

"Oh, umm, I was reading this ad about being an escort…", I began explaining.

"You both look a little young. Do you mind if I see some I.D.?", Jim interrupted.

We both pulled out our driver's license and showed them to him.

"Have either of you worked for an escort agency before?", he questioned.

"No.", again we said in unison.

"Well, we really cater to a more mature clientele and I'm just not sure how well it would work out for you guys?", Jim spoke as though he was about to turn us down.

I think he viewed us as young girls who didn't know what they were getting into.

"Wait. Listen Mr. Koen…"

"Call me Jim."

"Don't judge us by the way we're dressed. Sherry's in college and I scored in the 1200's on my SAT's. We can be sophisticated.", I argued.

"Don't get me wrong, I believe you can be, it's just….I'm not sure….", Jim hesitated to speak candidly.

"Oh, I know what it is. You're not sure if we really know what the game is", Sherry jumped in. "Well, we do!", Sherry finished by leaning over to me and tongue-kissing me as she lifted my shirt to expose my breasts to Jim.

After we'd completed an impromptu lez-show for him, Sherry said, "How is that? Do you believe we get it now?"

Jim's body shook with laughter before saying, "Oh I'm a believer now!".

"Okay so when can we start working?", Sherry continued driving the conversation. I just laid back recognizing she was doing better than I had.

"Saturday. I got a job that's perfect for what you just did. Discretion is paramount in our business. Our clients trust that their information will never be released. You'll have to sign confidentiality agreements first and then I've got a special assignment for the two of you!"

We both signed the agreement which had a clause that if we ever talked about a client or assignment we'd owe damages in the amount of $8-million dollars for breaking the agreement. Jim explained that the clause was to keep escorts from trying to sell what they'd done with famous clients for profit.

» » » » » » » » » » » » » » « « « « « « « « « « « « « «

We didn't get our assignment until that Saturday morning. It was one of my favorite rappers, *2-Nice*, who was performing a concert at the Georgia Dome in downtown Atlanta.

We stopped by the Elite Escorts office to pick-up our backstage passes and keys to our own hotel room at the luxurious Wyndham. This was the shit. Sherry and I couldn't believe we were gonna get paid $500 each to fuck *2-Nice*, who we would've fucked for free! Of course, Jim never used words like "fuck" or "sex", he would just tell us to "satisfy" the client, but we knew what he meant.

We were treated like royalty when we arrived at the security gates with our backstage passes. We met *2-Nice's* manager, Curtis, who escorted us to a private room where we could watch the concert on a huge big screen monitor, eat and drink champagne.

2-Nice was already preparing to go on stage, so we'd have to wait to meet him. During an intermission, Curtis came into our private room to make sure we were alright. We definitely were. Both of us were lovin' the baller-life.

Curtis talked in code just as much as Jim.

"Alright. I want y'all to be ready to take care of my man when the concert is over", he smiled at us.

"Oh, we're ready baby!", Sherry bragged walking over to him and kneeling down.

Sherry unzipped his pants, pulled out his *shit* and began sucking his dick right then and there. Following her lead, I knelt beside her and we alternated sucking his dick. At one point, I had his balls in my mouth as Sherry continued sucking his dick until he came on her face.

"Woooo, shit!", Curtis sighed after delivering a mega-nut. "I see you girls don't play!"

"No we some real ass bitches! We keeps it real, so let yo' boy *2-Nice* know the deal!", Sherry said talkin' so much shit that I wanted to slap her.

But apparently, Sherry knew what she was doing as Curtis laughed at her rhyming, pulled out a wad of money as thick as a *Subway* sandwich and peeled off two $100 bills for each of us.

Daaa-yum!!, I was thinking to myself. *$200 for a fuckin' blow-job. I gotta find a way to do this shit full-time.*

It pissed me off just to think about all the dicks I'd already sucked for free!

» » » » » » » » » » » » » » » « « « « « « « « « « « « « « «

After the concert, the night didn't go at all like I'd expected. We did get to meet *2-Nice*, briefly. Curtis introduced us to the shirtless sweating star who didn't even bother to look our direction. He just murmured, *Nice to meet you*, through a towel he was wiping sweat off his face with. Then we were ushered away and given instructions to go back to the hotel and he'd come by later.

It was nearly 4 a.m. when he finally showed up at our hotel room, flanked by two muscle-bound bodyguards.

2-Nice walked around the room like it was his and made himself comfortable on the sofa.

We didn't know what to say to him, as he didn't appear to be very cordial. So we just stood there waiting on instructions.

"Why are you hoes still in your clothes?", he questioned with his arms open.

I didn't like being called a ho, but what was I gonna do.

Sherry and I undressed quickly and started walking over to *2-Nice* to begin sexin' him.

"Hold the fuck up! *2-Nice* ain't told you to come over to him yet!", he irritatingly spoke in third-person.

"I don't know what we're s'pose to do?", I candidly commented.

"Moose, I'm so tired of Jim sending me these rookie-ass hoes", *2-Nice* spoke to one of his bodyguards. Then turned his attention back to us. "Y'all ain't nuttin' but hoes to *2-Nice*. You gotta suck my boyz' dicks first to see if you're worthy of *2-Nice*'s shit!"

Sherry and I looked at each other for a moment before kneeling down in front of *2-Nice*'s boys and sucking them both to orgasms as *2-Nice* watched.

We wiped our faces clean of the bodyguards' juices and simply looked in 2-Nice's direction, having learned not to assume anything with him.

"Alright both of you get on the bed.", he directed us.

We did as told without a word of rebuttal.

"Moose, get the bag.", he instructed.

Moose, the bodyguard, unzipped a black bag and emptied its contents on the bed. It was filled with all sorts of sex toys, dildos and shit.

"Thick chocolate, I want you to work on her.", *2-Nice* instructed without regard to actually finding out our names.

He was telling Sherry to sex me with the dildos. Sherry hesitated, wondering if it was alright with me. When I began positioning myself, Sherry knew it was okay.

Sherry started by sucking my nipples to concrete hardness and rubbing my pussy with her hand before accepting a vibrating dildo handed to her by Moose.

"Thick chocolate. That bitch better cum too!", *2-Nice* yelled across the room.

From the moment that vibrating dildo hit my clit I was already cumming. My body was shaking and twitching all over the place as the sensation was becoming a little too much.

The other bodyguard handed Sherry yet another dildo to insert in my pussy, while the vibrating one had me all rubbery. With a vibrator on my clit and a dildo pumping *in-n-out* of me, I was screaming in ecstasy in a high-pitched voice, as I could faintly hear the deep-voice laughter of approval of the bodyguards.

"And don't stop until I tell you to", shouted *2-Nice*.

I was already done and I thought Sherry should've known it, yet she continued to punish me with her fast-paced pumping. When *2-Nice* finally gave her the okay to stop, I was mad at how Sherry had done me. Even wondered if she was trying to *wear-me-out* on purpose, so that she could be the one to fuck *2-Nice*.

As I laid there breathing heavier than ever, light-head and completely exhausted, *2-Nice* granted me the opportunity to return the favor to Sherry, which I gladly did.

While I was busy giving her the same exact treatment as she'd given to me without regard to her crying-out that she was cumming, Moose suggested to *2-Nice* that I put a dildo in her ass.

As Sherry was turning over to a hands-n-knees position, she looked sternly at me, trying to indicate that I should take it easy on her, no matter what *2-Nice* said. Thinking about how she'd done me and wondering would she have taken it easy if they'd wanted me to get fucked in the ass, I came to the conclusion that she wouldn't have. So I didn't either. I had dildos in both holes at the same time, rapidly alternating *in-n-out* strokes Sherry was screaming "Please!" and her ass and thighs were waving like a battleship flag.

"Damn! Tall girl is off da chain!", *2-Nice* complimented my actions.

Finally, I pulled both dildos from Sherry, as she immediately fell to the bed laying on her side and using a finger to massage feeling back into her asshole.

2-Nice invited me over to him. I think Sherry was a little jealous, although she knew she was in no position to do anything more, thanks to me.

I straddled *2-Nice* in a Cow-Girl position and rubbed my pussy on him until I could feel his hardness through his jogging-suit pants.

I about *tripped* when I'd pulled his pants off, began *jacking-him-off* with my hand and he snapped his fingers at one of the bodyguards who scurried over with a condom, opened it up and actually put it on his dick for him. That was some strange looking shit!

I proceeded to fuck the shit out *2-Nice*. Had him whispering "slow down" in my ear, so he wouldn't look bad in front of his bodyguards by cumming too quickly. I played along by screaming loudly like his dick was the best thing since sliced bread, which he appreciated.

When he grunt-whispered that he was about to cum, I dismounted, pull his condom off and took all of his juices in mouth while staring him square in the eye.

"Whoooaaa. That bitch is baaddddd, *2-Nice*!", exclaimed the bodyguards.

It was odd, but being called a bitch didn't seem bad when they were using the word in a complimenting sentence.

"What's yo' name ma?", *2-Nice* asked showing he'd gained some respect for me.

"Mysterious", I said, as Moose was handing me a towel to use to wipe away some juice that had made out the corner of my mouth.

"I'ma have to get yo' number, girl!", *2-Nice* said smiling for the first time. "I don't leave town 'til Wednesday morning, I'ma call you, awight? You and me, we goin' go shoppin'!"

Then *2-Nice* reached in his pants peeled off a grand and handed it to me.

"That's for you Mysterious", he said, handing me the money.

He then peeled off $200 more and told me to give that to my girl, referring to Sherry. All the money he was giving was in addition to the money we were getting from *Elite Escorts.* I guess his money was the tip.

Up until that point, everyone had all but ignored Sherry's presence in the room.

I finished giving my phone number to Moose who stored it in his cell phone. *2-Nice* got dressed, gave me a hug and waved to Sherry before exiting our hotel room.

"That was the shit!", I said to Sherry, having waited for the hotel room door to close behind them.

"Yeah, whatever.", Sherry said sounding pissed.

"Aww, gurrll quit trippin'! You know we we're gonna split all the money equally!", I attempted to alleviate her concern about the disparity in money.

"I don't want your money! He gave that shit to you, just give me my $200!", Sherry charged as she was pulling up her jeans, apparently preparing to leave.

I didn't know why she was actin' all crazy. She knew we were putting on a show. Plus, I wasn't gonna let her make me feel bad. It wasn't like her ass wasn't trying to wear me out too. It ain't my fault that she couldn't last. Or that *2-Nice* was feelin' me and not her.

I couldn't believe Sherry actually left, instead of spending the night in our complimentary room.

Chapter Four A Way Of Life

On Monday, *2-Nice* had Moose call me to set-up a lunch date at *Justin's* on Peachtree. He had a limo sent to my apartment to pick me up and later we went shopping and spent a lot of his money on me at Lenox Mall.

Sherry and I still hadn't spoken since the night that we met *2-Nice*, which was unusual because we either saw or spoke to each other just about everyday.

I figured she was harboring a jealous grudge, but I called her Monday night anyway. I got her voicemail on the very first ring, which either meant that her cell phone wasn't turned on or that she'd pressed the ignore-button when she saw that it was me calling.

On Tuesday, I swung by the Georgia Perimeter College campus to find Sherry. We'd been *girlz* for too long for one night to ruin our friendship. When I finally caught up with her in the student-union area, she couldn't help but smile, though she tried to turn her face into looking unimpressed.

"What's up girl?", I questioned

"Nothing. I'm going to class.", Sherry replied.

"Don't even try it. I've been to the registrar's office, your next class ain't for another hour", I explained away the lame excuse Sherry tried to use to avoid talking with me. "Gurrll, you know we've been tight for too damn long for us to be actin' like 'dis over some nigga, I'on't care even if it is *2-Nice*!"

Sherry just stared at me. Didn't say a word. However, her stern hip-out posture was softening.

"I'ma let you go get ready for class, but I'm saying this: You are my best friend. And I hope that I'm still yours. Come by my place tonight so that we can work this shit out…please. I don't know where I could find a better friend than you! At least do that for me.", I finished with watery eyes.

As I leaned in to give her a hug, I was surprised that she accepted it. While hugging her I slid $400 into her purse without detection. In my eyes, that money was rightfully her share of the money we scored from *2-Nice*. Now we had split the $1200 that *2-Nice* had given equally, $600 each.

» » » » » » » » » » » » » » » » « « « « « « « « « « « « « « « «

Two years later, at age 21, Sherry and I were full-time in the baller-catching game. Sherry had dropped out of college because the money we were making sexin' ballers was much more than she'd ever start-out earning with her degree.

We were working our angles like pros. Experience was the mother of all teachers.

We still kept our gig with Elite Escorts, but it really wasn't necessary. We had devised our own strategies for meeting and using ballers. It did take some time to establish what we called our "Hook-Up Network".

Our *Hook-Up Network* was unrelated groups of people in key positions that would aid us in being in the right places at the right times to meet ballers. It included club-owners, concert promoters, pro-sports personnel, radio Dj's, hotel general managers, restaurant owners and more.

With this *Hook-Up Network* we were able to obtain backstage passes, invites to exclusive parties and tickets to every major concerts and sports events.

Though the *Hook-Up Network* did take time to establish, about 2-years for it to be totally complete, that was primarily the easy part. Getting those people to get us tickets and our names on the VIP-lists was as easy as fucking them. Though there were plenty of women out there that were trying to do the same, we had the advantage over them because Sherry and I worked as a team. No individual women could top our threesome sex acts. So we were always #1 with these guys when it came time to *Comp* us some tickets or passes. And, we never had to worry about trying to act like we were trying to be in a relationship with them to score the favors. We weren't the kind of girls they'd want as a girlfriend, anyway. They just wanted the sex fun and fantasy that we were providing and never grew tired of it.

The hardest part of the whole baller-catching game was to not get pimped or played for just the sex.

To be perfectly honest, that did happen to us a couple of times. Even beyond that, there was even more we had to learn about the game – stuff like who to fuck and how not to fuck.

» » » » » » » » » » » » » » » » « « « « « « « « « « « « « « « «

After attending one of the All-Star games, both Sherry and I each hooked-up with one of the All-Stars, courtesy of introductions through one of the people from our *Hook-Up Network.*

I knew right from the start that the basketball players were putting us into the category of a one-night stands. Not even wanting to take us to dinner before inviting us back to their separate hotel rooms. But we allowed our emotions to get the best of us and forgot that we're suppose to be in it for the money. I ain't talkin' 'bout getting paid for the sex like hookers. I'm talkin' 'bout giving the impression of a relationship so that we could get more later. That's where the real money lies.

In two separate rooms, with two different athletes, Sherry and I were making the same mistake.

They were our first athlete ballers. Both of them over 6'3 with sexy lean-muscular frames. When my athlete pulled his pants down and I saw that long-ass dick that rivaled a horses, I wanted to pick up the phone and call Sherry to tell her. Little did I know she was experiencing the same thing in her room.

That night, painfully I learned that it was important to know my limitations. I'd fucked him in all the wrong positions, giving him the chance to really put it on me, instead of being in positions to control him and his thang. Doggie-style was a very bad idea. Whew, I still shiver just thinking about that. And I don't know what the hell went through Sherry's mind when she allowed him to do anal sex with her. I mean, my choices were stupid, but hers was just down-right idiotic!

Meeting up with Sherry in the hotel lobby, both of us walked to our car like we'd just finished a four-day horseback ride through a rocky mountain trail. Both of us were *worn-the-fuck-out*! And with nothing to show for it. Not any money or even as much as a phone number from either one of them.

Later in the season, we cheered when both of their teams lost in the playoffs. Little in the form of revenge, but we held onto that anyway.

Sherry and I had made the conscious decision to never allow those kinds of mistakes to happen ever again! We sat at my dining room table with notepads and pens like U.S. War Strategists and mapped out a series of *do's* and *don'ts.*

In our minds, this was like a war. Our goal was to capture the enemy's (ballers) money and limit the amount of casualties. It was ironic because we even read through some of Sherry's old psychology books she still had from college to try to understand the human mind.

After getting our asses worn-out for free, we decided to take this shit seriously. We were committed to being the very best baller-catchers.

We knew where to meet the ballers. And had a way to get to them through our *Hook-Up Network.* But what we'd failed to do in the past was to have a formal strategy on how to get the baller's money.

In the past, the money just happened. Now we were developing strategies Sherry nicknamed *Baller-Catching 101*, that would ensure that our efforts would never be in vain.

One of the first rules we developed was that sex was never to be for enjoyment. It was for money, period.

As we reflected on what things had worked well in the past, we also talked about what hadn't. One of the major items was the one that was most fresh in our minds – what to do with big-dick ballers.

Though we talked about how we could handle them better if we brought them closer to orgasm by oral sex before allowing them to stick their dicks in us, thereby reducing the time we'd have to endure them, it still came down to being able to handle large dicks. And the only way to do that was practice. So we did...on each other.

We purchased large-ass dildos from a sex-novelty store on Memorial Drive in Stone Mountain and routinely fucked the shit out of each other with them, until our bodies had become accustomed to handling big dicks. It wasn't sexual, it was business.

While practice gained improvement with our body's ability to handle big dicks, it wasn't true with oral sex. No matter how much we practiced, both of us would lose control of ourselves, so we decided that we'd have to cut oral-sex out of the picture completely. Adding the "*Never Let A Baller Eat Your Pussy*" rule to the growing list of baller-catching procedures.

Something else we noticed was that when a baller was able to wear your ass out in bed, they didn't feel the need to do it again. It was as though they conquered or achieved their goal and it was time for them to move-on to someone else.

Another rule we wrote down was to always make a baller spend money on us before fucking them. We didn't care if it was as small as paying for dinner, but something to keep them from treating us totally as *hoes*. That way, we'd be able to keep contact and be able to run game on him later.

In all, we developed and tested countless strategies to make baller-catching easier. So much so, over our hoochie-mama outfits we felt like we should be wearing scientist lab coats. We were that sophisticated in our research. Even at one of our regular weekly brain-storming sessions, we teased about how we'd collected so much information that we'd be able to write a book and call it *Sex A Baller*. But then we thought, how would we sell it?

As a part of our plan, we enlisted Jim Koen from Elite Escorts to become our official *Sex-Test Dummy*. We tried all types of sex on him and went as far as to write down the results, like what he seemed to like the most, what made him cum fastest and all sorts of other things. Of course, he was unaware that we were just using him and wouldn't have cared if we'd told him anyway. To him, he was just getting free pussy.

In addition to sexing Jim for research purposes, we parlayed it into stepping-up in the game by getting him to help us diversify our baller portfolios. Knowing that we could already reach entertainment and athlete ballers, we convinced him to give us assignments with corporate clients, CEOs and people like that.

We also did our own diversification without Jim's help. Sherry was a *Thugaholic* and chose to hang with Street Ballers. I was getting more into the Business and Investment Ballers.

Remembering how much Mr. Peterson would pay to not have his infidelity get back to his wife, I looked for the married ballers. For me it was just easier. They weren't looking for a relationship, therefore wouldn't be upset because I had other ballers. And if we ever *fell-out*, I could continue getting the benefits with the threat of telling their wife. Of course, I never would tell their wife. That'd be like killing the golden goose.

I tried to convince Sherry to join me in taking this path, but she was hooked on going after the Thug-Ballers. Time and time again, I warned her that it was a dangerous game she was playing. But she wouldn't listen to me, not even after she spent a night in jail when the police stopped a car she was riding in and they found drugs in the car.

It wasn't until she got the beat-down of her life from this guy named Dynamite, who was a local drug dealer and gang leader. Sherry always had the propensity to talk a lot of shit, but she had to learn who she could do that shit with. Dynamite wasn't havin' it!

Though I hated seeing her swollen and bruised, I was glad that the beat-down had brought her back to her senses before she got killed.

We were making plenty of money at the time, running our games on ballers, anywhere from $1,000 to $1,500 a week. I couldn't understand why she'd ever put that in jeopardy for a damn hoodlum. But some of us just have to learn that way, I guess.

Chapter Five Payback Is A MoFo

Three years later, Sherry and I were neighbors in a ritzy black community called *The Cascades* in East Atlanta. Old-money lived there. New-school entrepreneurs. Entertainers and all sorts of other rich folks.

At a little over 25, both of us were the youngest people to own a house on our block. And our old-money neighbors hated us. We threw parties that went late into the night and watered our lawn in skimpy shorts and tank tops without bras, just to piss them off more. We didn't feel bad about it either, 'cause our neighbors would call the City of Atlanta to report any and every little thing that was wrong with our property.

Just a year or so earlier, I made fun of Sherry because she was *gaming* a 68 year-old white man she'd met at Grady Memorial Hospital while visiting a sick aunt.

How in the hell do you fuck a man that old?, I'd often ask her. I even would come up with nicknames for her or make comments that I knew would piss her off. I'd call her the "Viagra Princess of Hip-Hop" or ask her if she was gonna do *'69'* as a Birthday gift when he turned 69.

To be honest, I thought her ass was being as stupid as she was when she decided to curse out a drug-dealing gang leader. But, I had to admit that I was wrong.

It turned out that the old man had no family and when he died, he'd willed both houses he owned and had been renting-out to Sherry in return for the attention she'd paid to him during his last year.

Upon getting the deeds to the property, Sherry quickly gave the families that had resided in the homes for the past two years a 60-day notice that they had to move-out and then we moved in. I'm sure that contributed to our neighbors hostility towards us, besides the fact that I think the older women were just jealous because we looked good.

I told Sherry that we should live in one house and she should rent the other. But she had other plans. Just as I'd done with *2-Nice's* gift, Sherry signed over the deed to me on the other house. I couldn't believe it. So there we were, 25 year-old baller-catching *Cascades*-residing home-owners.

We kept-on baller catching so that we could maintain our lifestyles. We had the best custom furniture from *Seigels* on Peachtree Street. Flat-screen televisions, I had two in my house. And neither one of us cooked or cleaned, so we spent a lot of money going out to eat and sharing a housekeeper that came by twice a week.

Now that we were a little older, we found that we actually had to work-out to keep our shapes. I know I had taken my body's ability to automatically burn-off calories for granted, until one-day that all changed. No longer could I just eat anything without regard to gaining weight. And Sherry was a short brickhouse, so she definitely needed to stay in the gym. Quite easily she could go from *stacked* to *stumpy* within as little as a week's time. But neither one of us was ever gonna let that happen. Baller-catching was our careers.

We joined *Silhouette*, an exclusive gym not far from our expressway exit off I-20. Four times a week, we were there. After hiring a personal trainer, Renard, I believed we actually looked better than we did when we were 21. Our muscles were now toned and had more definition.

» » » » » » » » » » » » » » » « « « « « « « « « « « « « « «

Each of us now had several ballers in our portfolio. The latest one that I'd added was Remington Charles, a 46 year-old corporate executive at a major Fortune-500 company based in Atlanta.

He was a debonair looking man that appeared no older than 35 or 36. Just a twinkle of gray on his side-burns was the only clue that he might be older. A Penn University graduate, he'd been in Atlanta less than a week when we met at *The Tavern* a semi-upscale restaurant in Buckhead.

Remington was brought here from his company's New York offices to be the new President of Sales and Marketing. The very first black President of a division in his company's history.

At *The Tavern*, when I began flirting, Remington made it no secret that he was married. His wife and family were still living back in *The Hamptons* until the house the company had built for him in Atlanta was ready. When I told him that I didn't care that he was married, I could tell he was still *down* with us going out.

Even before his family moved from New York to Atlanta, I was the first woman he'd sexed in their bed. It did feel a little funny knowing that I'd seen the finished house before the wife did.

Most of our contact after his family moved here happened at my house, unless he was going out of town on a business trip. In that case, Remington would book me on the same flight as him and we'd spend 2 or 3 days together, usually in New York.

The best part about *gaming* Remington was that I don't think he cared. I believe he knew why I was with him, but figured he was getting *his*, so why muddy the water with expectations.

Another reason I enjoyed being around him was because he was so intelligent. I learned business terms and principles just by listening to him talk about what was going on at his company.

The only thing that bothered me was that I was lying to him about what I did for a living. To explain my 2-story, 3-bedroom, 2-car garage home, I told him that my deceased aunt had left it to me. As far as how I was making living-expense money, I told him that I worked part-time as a model.

The lies were piling-up very high mainly because he was so inquisitive. Normally I wouldn't give a shit about lying to a baller. But for some reason, I had a special admiration for him. And I think he felt the same way about me. Often he'd encourage me to look into going to college. Even offered to get me a job at his company. Also, he said that he could pull some strings to get my schooling paid through a Tuition-Reimbursement program that the company offered.

I hated when he talked about my possible future career options, partly because it made me feel bad about my current career. I usually quieted him by asking about his wife or family. That would get him to change the subject in a hurry.

» » » » » » » » » » » » » » » » « « « « « « « « « « « « « « « «

Sherry was also *gaming* a new baller, Miguel Santiago, an heir to a chain of vacation resorts in Mexico.

Sherry and I spent a vacation weekend at one the resorts Miguel's family owned and that's how they met.

Walking along the sandy beach in tiny swimsuits shielded only by the shear wraps we wore, Sherry and I attracted a lot of whistles and attention. Especially, Sherry with that big ass of hers.

While we were making our way up the slight-incline sandy beach hill that led back to the hotel, Miguel was shirt-less lying on a towel on the beach. His honey-brown body glistened in the warm sun like Latin-gold that neither one of us missed the opportunity to glance at through our sun-glasses.

Miguel was definitely a sexy Latin lover who was as charming as they come with his gorgeous accent, endearing smile and wavy jet-black hair. At 6'2, 200-lbs, Miguel's body was tan and toned to perfection. It was like he was the Hispanic version of Morris Chestnut.

As we approached, he sat up at attention, equally as intrigued to study our frames as we sashayed by. After we'd passed by, we were too busy leaning into each other whispering words like *Damn! That boy was fine!*, to notice that he'd gotten off the towel to follow us.

"Excuse me?", we heard a voice with a spanish accent say.

As we both turned around, found-out that the melodious voice belonged to the Latin-god-like-creature we'd just walked past, I knew we both had the same thought in our minds. *Who is he interested in?*

"I don't mean to bother you. I just wanted to introduce myself to you guys. I'm Miguel Santiago.", he spoke with a rolling tongue that already had me daydreaming what else he could do with that tongue.

"I'm Mysterious and this is my friend Sherry.", I spoke while extending my hand trying to draw the attention to me.

Sherry knew what I was doing and gave me a gentle sly elbow to let me know that she knew to as we tried to out-blush each other.

"Mysterious and Sherry, what beautiful names.", he said by accepting and kissing the back of each of our hands.

Being a baller-catcher, reading clues was very necessary. And I'd become very good at it. In the quick instant it took for him to kiss our hands, I knew that it was Sherry that he was interest in. The average woman may not have noticed it, but he'd kissed Sherry's hand a fraction of a second longer.

In horse-racing they call it losing by a nose, in my case, I think I was edged out by her ass. Had he not had to catch-up with us from behind, I think I may've had a better chance. I believe he'd made his decision on his way to us by comparing our asses. I guess, you lose some and you win some.

Later that evening, inside of a nightclub that was located in the hotel, I got a chance to see Miguel's sexy body rhythmically moving on the dance floor with Sherry. Surprisingly, Miguel's dance skills were not limited to that of when Latin music was playing. The boy could dance just as well to hip-hop music. He had an urban flare to him he must've obtained while attending and graduating from Rutgers University.

» » » » » » » » » » » » » » » » « « « « « « « « « « « « « « « «

I have to admit, I was a little jealous of Sherry's across-the-border baller hook-up. She'd be treated to sunny beach vacations any time she wanted. And after watching the way Miguel's chiseled body moved and swayed on the dance floor, especially his lower body, I knew she was getting some of the very best Latin-dick too!

» » » » » » » » » » » » » » » » « « « « « « « « « « « « « « « «

Later that same year, Sherry and I were at yet another All-Star event. At an invitation-only gala held in a convention room at the hotel where we were staying, we ran into none other than the same basketball players that had played us three years earlier.

The fact that they actually remembered us, I didn't know how to take that. Was it because they'd remembered how stupid we were or was there something special about us? If I were betting, I'd have to put my money on the first one.

Though we'd improved greatly, thanks to the strategies we'd developed, that encounter should have been *water-under-the bridge* and we were still smarting from it.

At least this time when we met, the players offered to buy us drinks as we found a private table in the corner of the room.

When Sherry and I excused ourselves to the ladies room, we couldn't resist a plan for revenge. It had nothing to do with money. It was all about the redemption of pride, the recovery of dignity and our desire to avenge a defeat.

As expected, our benign conversation was turned, by them, into an invitation to their hotel room across the street. Instead, we decided to make them come upstairs to our room. It was just a power play.

Once inside the room, Sherry and I played coy no more, immediately undressing them. Our aggressiveness took them a little by surprise, but they weren't complaining. We matched up with the same guy that we had 3 years earlier.

Sherry pushed her athlete onto the bed and had him lying on his back as she was sucking the hell out of his dick. I was doing the same, only kneeling in front of my guy by the sofa.

Using a method we developed and tested on Jim Koen called the *Two-Hand Jack*, I could hear both men panting heavily.

"Ooo, shit. Hold on a minute. Wait.", my guy was starting to plead because of the incredible sensation I'd created quickly. At the same time, I heard Sherry's guy say, "Slow down. Damn!".

Neither one of us adhered to their requests, as we quickly peeked at each other before gripping their dicks tighter and hand-stroking them fast until they both came.

I ain't gonna lie, we enjoyed the hell out of watching their humbled and embarrassed faces. And reveled in the fact that we'd turned their asses out so fast. To further add insult to injury, we struggled condoms on their quickly softening dicks and told them we wanted to be fucked now. We knew that they couldn't do it right at that moment. We just wanted them to feel bad about it.

My guy tried to hide the fact that his dick was limp by attempting to buy himself some time by placing me on the floor as he lowered his head to perform oral on me. Remembering one of our baller-catching rules, I placed my hands under his chin to prevent his tongue from even getting close to my pussy.

"Uhn-uhn. I want you to fuck me.", I said with a devilish grin to him.

Sherry had done similar to her guy, as she turned over to her hands and knees, raising her irresistible plump derriere up to position herself for Doggie-style sex while telling him to fuck her now.

Turning my head to the side, I could see Sherry's guy holding his limp-ass dick in his hand nervously and frantically shaking it, trying to bring it back to life.

When I turned my attention back to my guy, I saw that he was doing the same. Though he was able to negotiate a penetration of sorts, his dick kept slipping out because of its lack of hardness.

"Damn. C'mon. I'm waiting.", I taunted him with my fingers interlocked behind my head like I was just chillin'.

I enjoyed his failure to give a rebuttal comment. There was nothing he could say.

Sherry's guy managed to penetrate her as well, but was having the same problem with keeping it in.

Following my lead, Sherry unmercifully taunted her guy as well.

"Forget that. I want you to fuck my ass.", she chanted while using her own hands to spread her butt cheeks.

She knew damn well that he would need rock-hardness to be able to penetrate the smaller hole. It was her way of winning the rematch because last time he'd worn her ass out.

I couldn't help but giggle at that point. Watching that boy's face that showed he wanted to fuck that ass so bad, I think he was about to cry, was very funny. A juicy booty was staring him in the face and he could do nothing with it.

He made several comical attempts to penetrate Sherry's ass with his limp dick. But with each try, his dick folded-up like an accordion. Out of frustration, he cheated, trying to gain back some of the sex-power by sliding a finger in her ass instead. Little did he know, we were not the same girls as last time. Sherry had practiced and prepared for this situation, so she was able to calmly take his finger insertion while placing her hand under her chin as though she were bored and looked back at him with a glance as if to say, "*Is that suppose to do something? Am I suppose to be screaming in ecstasy because you got a finger in my butt?*". Her ability to handle it created more frustration.

"I didn't say that I wanted you to fuck my ass with your finger.", calmly she commented calling into question as to why he didn't use his dick.

Ruthless and relentless was how we treated them, but hey, that's how they'd done us.

"Y'all gotta go. I'ma fuck my girl so I can get more satisfaction.", I ended their torture with a final insult to their egos.

"Fuck you bitches!", my guy said as he was getting dressed.

"No. The point is, neither one of you could FUCK these bitches! That's the point. We wished you lame ass niggas could've FUCKED '*these bitches*', then we wouldn't have to do it ourselves! So get yo shit and get out and let us do the man's job for you!", Sherry jumped in with much attitude.

After they left, we both felt vindicated. We laughed and recounted the events that just happened like they'd taken place years and years ago.

Chapter Six California Dreamin'

A year later, I'd graduated from regular ballers to celebrity ones. Movie stars, television hosts, comedians and a host of others.

I was spending a lot of my time in Los Angeles, California, about 1-2 weeks every month. The money the Cali-ballers spent was incredible because they just had it like that.

Sherry would sometimes accompany me to California, but she hadn't hooked on to a celebrity baller yet. Though, I did do my best to introduce her to friends of my ballers. Out in Cali, the stars didn't have an appreciation for Sherry's thick shape, like just about the rest of the country. They liked a little shape, but most often preferred the long, lean type – more like white girls. And that definitely was not Sherry.

L.A. is certainly a place that marches to a different beat. It takes some adjusting to, but once you have its rhythm, a baller-catcher can do extremely well.

My latest baller victim was a very well-known 30-something actor, who I'll call Kevin Jones, to protect the innocent. Kevin wasn't as tall as he appeared on screen, but every bit as sexy. At just 5'10" tall, which ain't really that short, I just prefer taller men, his body was extremely cut with virtually no body fat.

I'd met Kevin in Atlanta during a shooting of his newest film. Both Sherry and I had been hired as *extras* in the movie, courtesy again of our *Hook-Up Network.*

When our eyes met outside of his movie-set trailer, I knew that I had Kevin. I don't know how to explain it, but it was something about the intensity in his eyes.

Surprisingly he wasn't arrogant like I'd've expected from a star of his stature. But once I learned that he was originally from Alabama, then it made since why he seemed grounded. Though I never would of guessed he was from Alabama 'cause he didn't even have a hint of a southern accent.

Once filming had wrapped-up we went out to dinner, the night before he was flying back to California. It was a relatively non-eventful night. He was tired and dreading his early-morning flight back to L.A., as he was scheduled to appear on the *Jay Leno Show* the following evening.

Watching him on *Jay Leno*, I hated that I didn't get a chance to sex him. He was looking so good, full of charm and energy on the show!

On our brief date, I'd thrown every hint possible, but he never responded. I wasn't sure if it was the fatigue from the 3-months of film shooting that made him not reciprocate, or if it was that he wasn't feeling me? But, by the end of the date, I assumed it was the fatigue because he did ask for my phone number.

I'd all but forgotten about him when he *out-of-the-blue* called me three months later. We talked on the phone for four nights in a row before he invited me to come to California -- on his dime of course.

I told him that I felt uncomfortable coming out there by myself. I didn't really. I was just testing him to see what I could get, trying to *get-over* a little.

It worked. He sprung for 1st-class plane tickets and hotel accommodations for me and Sherry.

We spent a large portion of the 5-days that we'd be in California as tourists, visiting different sights. Kevin invited his 3-years younger brother, Chris, to come along, so not to have Sherry feel like a third wheel.

Chris was just as sexy as Kevin and I think could've been as successful in the movies.

Sherry was feeling him as her eyes widened when they were first introduced. However, I think Chris had been out in L.A. too long and had lost his appreciation for black women. He sounded and acted more like a pseudo white-boy, which made me and Sherry shake our heads because we thought it was a shame that such a fine black man would be confused.

After four days of showing hospitality for Sherry's sake, Kevin wanted to get me alone the night before we were to leave. Sherry just hung-out at the hotel, as Kevin and I embarked on our second date in 4-months.

We went to a Middle-Eastern restaurant in the tiny rich community of Brentwood. It was strange because he wasn't getting harassed like he normally did when we'd gone other places. I guess the rich folks in this area weren't impressed that a star was in their midst. I was sure they see them all the time, so it was no big deal. Though a camera crew from the television show *Celebrities Uncensored* was taking video of us as we walked to the car that the valet had just driven to us. They addressed him by name and asked if I was his girlfriend. Kevin was un-frazzled by their intrusion and even knew some of them by name, though he didn't even attempt to explain who I was. Instead he just smiled, shook their hands as he shielded me from them with his body as the valet assisted me to climbing into his Hummer-H2.

As we drove off, Kevin unnecessarily apologized.

"Mysterious I'm sorry about that. I really am. I didn't think that they'd be at that restaurant.", he said.

"Oh don't worry about it. Now I can tell my friends to look for me on *Celebrities Uncensored.* It's better than being on *Jenny Jones*!", I joked, trying to ease his sense of responsibility.

"I'm glad that you're not mad. A lot of people think that an actor's life is full of attention and it's all great. But sometimes you just wanna be left alone, you know?", he confessed.

"I feel you.", I said as though I empathized. But really I was thinking, *Shit, you give me millions of dollars and I wouldn't give a damn who takes my picture! I'd be the one saying 'cheese'!*

"Would you mind if we went to my house?", he quietly asked.

"That'd be nice", I said trying not to sound over-anxious.

We drove down Wilshire Boulevard until we reached the 405-expressway and drove north on I-101 on our way up into the Hollywood Hills section.

I was trippin' looking at the mansions as we drove through winding roads. I couldn't imagine anyone who could afford to live in a place like this.

Arriving at his large 12-bedroom, $23-million mansion, we pulled through the gated entrance that he'd used a remote control to open and parked at the front entrance of the estate that featured a circular cobblestone drive with a water-fountain in the middle of it.

I was so turned on right then, my nipples were hard and my panties wet.

Before he'd put the gear-shift in park, I'd already made up my mind that I was gonna fuck this nigga tonight whether he wanted to or not!

We were met by the estate valet, who took the keys and parked the H2 in the garage located around the rear of residence.

We were greeted in the huge marble-floored foyer, that was so large that our voices echoed, by Sergio the butler, well that's what I called him. I think they used another term like "Estate Coordinator" or some shit like that. He's a butler to me.

"Good evening Mr. Jones. Good evening, mam.", Sergio addressed both of us in a very proper manner.

"Quit it Sergio.", Kevin teased back to Sergio with a smile. "He always does that whenever someone he doesn't recognize is over the house", Kevin then explained to me before introducing us.

Apparently, Kevin wasn't one that wanted the aristocrat servitude that his Hollywood-residing peers so desired. But Sergio played the role, just in case I was someone from the industry that needed to be impressed. Once Kevin had made it clear that I wasn't from the industry, Sergio's voice changed from an almost regal British sound to that of a man from East L.A.

"How you doin' today?", he spoke to me in a commoner's voice.

I just laughed, "I'm fine."

I thought the little game they had going was both funny and cool.

Though they had an understanding and Kevin treated Sergio more like his boy than his butler, I could tell that Sergio didn't take advantage of it by failing in his duties.

"Kevin, did you want me to have some food prepared for you and Mysterious?", Sergio asked with concern.

"Naw man, we're cool, I think.", Kevin responded, looking to me to see if I wanted something. "Well, maybe you can bring us some popcorn in the movie room."

"As you wish masseur.", Sergio said with a sly grin, slight bow and a wink. He did so, to make Kevin feel a little embarrassed in front of me, now that we were all in on the joke.

"Get out of here, man!", Kevin teasingly shoved Sergio away like he was his roommate and not his employee.

We spent the rest of the evening in a gorgeous movie room the size of hotel conference room. Yet, it didn't feel too large. It was sectioned-off very nicely to create intimate spaces and decorated to the hilt. Beautiful tan fluffy carpet covered the floor. The carpeting was nothing like what I'd ever seen before, almost felt like a bear skin rug. Of course, he advised me to remove my shoes.

The room had a huge TV screen that dropped from the ceiling by remote and was about the height of me. Vintage film posters decorated the walls, some of them autographed by other actors.

Kevin made us some drinks as we made ourselves comfortable on the incredibly over-sized custom sofa that was as long as the height of three adults. I believed Kevin said that the sofa seated 10 people.

"How did an Alabama man get to being a big movie star.", I was to damn curious to not ask.

From my baller-catching experience, I knew better than to act like I was *jockin'* him, but I was blown away by everything and my curiosity got the better of me.

"Well, I started out modeling. I did some commercials and later auditioned for a small movie role. Things just took-off from there.", Kevin explained using the short version.

It wasn't the kinda conversation he wanted to go far into, so he politely just gave me an answer. Coming back to my senses and my purpose for being here, I chose not to follow-up with more questions in that area.

Instead, we relaxed on the mega-sofa that was long enough for Shaquille O'neal to get a good night's sleep on, ate popcorn and watched music videos.

I really got a chance to see the funny-side of Kevin that night as he'd do imitations of the music video moves, the funniest imitation being when he mimicked Beyoncè's quick butt-shaking move in her new *Crazy In Love* video.

"Uh-oh, uh-oh, uh-oh, oh-oh", Kevin chanted while standing shaking his *money-maker*.

That shit had me on the floor with laughter. He wasn't doing it horribly, but it wasn't what I'd expected from an actor who'd played such suave roles in film.

It did get me to take notice of how nice a butt he did have and I was determined to make him notice mine as I stood up to correct his dance form.

"It's not like that. It goes like this.", I said as I stood up and began my own imitation of Beyoncè's dance.

I could see in his face, the clowning had stopped as he saw me doing the booty-shaking move very well.

Kevin walked over to me amidst my gyrations and wrapped his hands around my waist and began kissing me the way I'd seen him do to his leading ladies in the movies. I delayed my tongues immediate swirling to play the good girl role a bit.

During that kiss, his hands were just as busy touring around my ass the way we'd toured L.A. the past few days.

I pulled his shirt off to reveal his *cut-up* body and kissed his chest slowly and gently. When he slid the straps on my halter top down my arms until my breasts were fully exposed, he sucked a nipple so hard into his mouth, I thought he intended to swallow it.

My pussy was the wettest it'd every been after he'd given fair and equal treatment to the other nipple.

I raised his head away from my breasts, with a hand under his chin, guiding him to standing erect and resume kissing me.

I transitioned from tongue kissing back to kissing his heavenly pectoral muscles on his chest, occasionally gliding a tongue across his nipples. Seductively, I began kissing down the front of his body, lower and lower, until I was at his waist-line and kneeling on the soft carpet.

I looked up at him, as I began taking off his belt and opening his pants. His dick was just beginning to get hard and it was just as pretty as his face. I placed it in my mouth as he played with my hair.

Kevin stood me up, using his hand's underneath-my-chin method as he undressed me while I was standing.

After he'd slid on a condom, I was dedicated to fucking the hell out of him. Sherry and I had established rules about not getting pregnant by certain types of ballers. But after witnessing the way he was living, I might've tried had he not chosen to use a condom.

I was aggressive right from the start, wrestling him to the plush-carpeted floor. I mounted him in *Cow-Girl* position, with his back on the floor, me on top and facing him. I slid his very good-size dick all the way inside me, which made my eyes water, tightly pinched his nipples and began intensely rowing my hips.

I slapped my butt up and down on his balls, as I heard him grunt with each slap. Even reached behind me and firmly gripped his balls while continuing to bucking up and down. After several minutes of riding him, I'd already made myself cum twice. But I didn't care. I was gonna get his nut, no matter what the cost to myself.

"Ohhhh, Mysterious.", he finally relented.

"Don't you cum yet", I teased back, as I dropped it all the way down on him and grinded my hips like I had a hula-hoop around my waist.

"Ohhh, Mysterious.", he again exclaimed.

"Not yet, I said. I'll let you know when you can cum!", I charged, doing a little tough-girl role-playing.

I watched his face squinting as he was trying not to disobey my orders by holding back inevitable ecstasy.

Not wanting to push him beyond himself, I slid down off of him with his legs inside of mine, pulled the condom off and began stroking his dick with my hand. I could feel his legs beginning to shake along the inside of my thighs shortly before he erupted in a form that rivaled the water fountain outside. His orgasm gushed like a geyser all over the front of me, in volumes I'd never seen before. It was everywhere – my hands, face, torso and hair.

Shit! How much cum did this brother release, a cups-worth? Damn, did I put it on him that good?!, I wondered to myself.

This was definitely some shit I knew I was gonna have to share with Sherry. It was that unbelieveable!

As it turned out, Sherry would have to wait two weeks to get the blow-by-blow details, as I decided to stay in California a little longer at Kevin's request.

Kevin and I were constantly together, so I didn't have a chance to give her the juice. I could've called in a restaurant bathroom to avoid Kevin's ear, but it wasn't the kinda story that I wanted to rush details. And besides, we were in Hollywood and Kevin was a star – you never know who might be hearing the details in the bathroom. So, I used my judgment that I should just wait.

During the additional two-week stay, I'd found that Kevin had a freaky-streak in him as well. He was an ass-slapping, sex-toy using wild sex animal. And I liked it!

I was even a co-star in our own little private sex porn-movie videotaped by Sergio, that we'd later watch on his big screen. And, I wasn't the first in his private home sex-movie collection. One evening before we had sex again, he pulled out a tape for us to watch of him with a famous female movie-star doing *the nasty*.

Kevin was much wilder than his public relations image.

Chapter Seven Remember Da Game

When I got back from L.A., Remington felt a little bit neglected because I'd spent so much time in California, which I found amusingly ironic because he had a wife. But still I knew that I'd have to appease him by sexing his feelings of neglect away.

» » » » » » » » » » » » » » » « « « « « « « « « « « « « « «

Though I'd only been gone for a few weeks, it seemed like I'd been gone for months. The recent news was that Sherry had hooked-up with a dirty-south recording artist. She'd always had a weak-spot for thugs, especially southern-thugs and he fit the bill perfectly. I knew who he was and more importantly his reputation. Sherry and I disagreed about the fact that I thought she was allowing herself to get to close to him without getting much in return.

"Sherry! We're baller-catchers! Remember that shit? Huh?", I screamed at her one evening trying to shake her back to her senses.

"I know that. That's what I'm doing.", she tried to defend herself.

"Bullshit, Sherry. If you playin' him then show the money!", I said borrowing a line from the movie, *Jerry Maguire*.

"I'm still setting him up, damn!", Sherry explained.

"You been fuckin' that nigga for two-weeks and you ain't got shit from him yet?! No jewelry, no money, no nothin' and you tryin' to tell me that you're setting him up?", sarcastically I responded.

"What about you Mysterious, all you did was fuck a star and stay your ass out in Hollywood eatin' Tofu and shit like that. Where's the money you were s'pose to be getting? Huh?", Sherry challenged, trying to change the subject.

I went to my purse and pulled out a roll of cash totaling $8,000 that Kevin had given me to cover any revenues that I might've missed by staying in L.A. for two weeks longer than I originally had planned.

I threw the money on the table as evidence.

"There's my baller-catcher loot. Where's yours?", candidly I taunted her.

Sherry cracked a smile, out of both pride for my accomplishment and in concession of the argument that she knew she'd just lost.

"Aw, fuck you, bitch. You ain't shit!", she laughed.

"You know I'm *The Shit*, right! Say it – Mysterious is the shit!", I played back with her.

"Fuck you ho.", Sherry teasingly waved me off with a quick hand-flip.

The same way that I'd studied baller tendencies and weaknesses, I knew Sherry's weakness very well – thugs. I don't know why, but she seemed to lose her damn mind around them and make mistakes.

I felt that it was my duty to be her baller-catcher reminder.

» » » » » » » » » » » » » » » « « « « « « « « « « « « « « «

I was trippin' when Remington invited me over to his house way-out in Kennesaw, Georgia. It wasn't like I hadn't been there before, but it was the fact that his wife would be home.

It was a fantasy of his he explained to have his mistress meet his wife without her being aware of who I really was.

It was some strange shit that tested the limits of my baller-catcher mentality. I didn't wanna do it, but then what kinda baller-catcher would I be if I vetoed a baller's fantasy. And while I'd always appreciated Remington's candor and honesty, which made it clear what we were both getting out of our relationship, some shit is better left alone.

In any case, I agreed to come by the house for dinner.

"Hello. I'm Lisa. It's very nice to meet you Keisha.", Remington's surprisingly beautiful early-30's wife greeted me with a smile at the door.

Remington had told his wife that my name was Keisha. I was supposedly one of his co-workers nieces that was job-hunting at his company. His co-worker was out-of-town and asked Remington to *look-after* me.

For some reason, I had pictured her as being as old as him, ugly and overweight. Otherwise, why would he need to cheat with me? Lisa was far from ugly. She was tall, had a pretty face, well-endowed in front and fashionably dressed in a long wrap-skirt that showed that *baby had back.* It was clear in that moment that Remington's need for me was more about the thrill of getting away with something.

I was so surprised that Remington was so comfortable playing this dangerous game that he didn't even come to the door until called by his wife.

"Hi, I'm Remington, you must be Keisha?", Remington spoke to me so convincingly so that I almost felt like we'd never met.

I was nervous as hell and had to shake-off my feelings of guilt as Lisa gave me a tour of the house and told me that I could help myself to anything that I wanted. Little did she know, I already had.

Judging by Remington's facial expressions as Lisa attempted to make me at ease in their house, I believed Remington actually enjoyed watching me being uncomfortable.

At dinner, I figured that Remington's children were from a previous marriage. First, because they didn't look at all like Lisa. Secondly, because they seemed too old for Lisa to have given birth to, as the boy was 12 and the girl was 9. Lisa couldn't have been more than 30 or 31. And finally, because they called her "Lisa" and called him "dad".

Though I had feelings of guilt, Lisa and I seemed to have a connection. Everything we talked about, clothes, music, movies – we both could relate to immediately. I didn't know why. I thought it might be because we were so close in age that we related better to each other than even to Remington. She even appeared to relate to him more like he was her uncle than her husband. It was sort of strange, but I just assumed it was because he was 15-years her senior.

I hated that I liked her. She had a special flare that was becoming. Lisa was a wife and now mother of Remington's pre-teen children, yet she still looked sexy with a wrap-skirt and matching top that was worn high enough to show her belly button on her flat stomach. On top of all of that, she was still active in her modeling career.

» » » » » » » » » » » » » » » « « « « « « « « « « « « « « «

Later that night, Remington and I were suppose to meet at the Peachtree Plaza Hotel for buck-wild sex.

We did meet there as planned. He was horny as hell having achieved his weird-fantasy goal of having me and Lisa meet. But I'd been impacted. I didn't wanna feel the way that I did. But I did.

"Come on, Mysterious, what's up?", Remington questioned at my lack of enthusiasm as he attempted to feel me up.

"I'on't know. It just doesn't feel right tonight.", I said back not wanting to admit to him or myself that I wasn't in the mood because I'd met his wife.

"Why? Because of Lisa?", he plainly asked.

"Not really.", I said, hating to think that I might actually be getting soft in my baller-catching attitude.

"Mysterious. It's Lisa, I know it. Look that's normal to feel that way, but once you let it go, trust me, the fact that you met her will turn into fun. I know, that's why I wanted you to come over", Remington said freely, showing me for the first time how cold he was capable of being.

Fuckit!, I thought to myself, attempting to will away feelings of guilt attached to having just met his wife a few hours ago.

However, the feelings kept making their way back into my mind as I was sucking his dick. So, I decided to appease him and keep my sanity at the same time. Gave him the All-Star Baller's treatment. Two-Hand Jack'd him into cumming quickly. It allowed me to give him the orgasm he'd come to the hotel for and in some way made me feel like I'd not actually sexed him 'cause there was no intercourse.

» » » » » » » » » » » » » » » « « « « « « « « « « « « « « «

"Girl, quit trippin'! You're a baller-catcher and he's a baller, that's it!", Sherry tried to convince me after I'd confided my feelings.

"Yeah, but she's really......", I attempted to interjection.

"She's really what? She's really not takin' care of business at home, that's what she is! That ain't your fault – that's hers! I mean, c'mon Mysterious, you're always the one telling me to keep my mind in the game. Now you're slippin'! If I felt that way, I'd just fuck him that much harder until that shit went away. That's all you gotta do!", Sherry said with fire in her voice.

"I know. You're right.", I admitted, though not quite totaling feeling good.

"That's what I'm talkin' 'bout! Shit. You had me worried about you for a minute. We Baller-Catcher fo' life!", Sherry cheered.

I needed that pep-talk and from all people, Sherry. She was the one that most often veered from the rules we'd created. But, I was glad that she was able to be there for me and get my ass back on track.

» » » » » » » » » » » » » » » « « « « « « « « « « « « « « «

A couple of days later, Sherry and I were together at our weekly hair-n-nails appointment at the beauty salon.

Both of us sitting side-by-side underneath a hair-dryer, when I noticed Lisa walking in with some guy that had his hand around her waist.

"Sherry, Sherry, Sherry!", I said frantically tapping her leg with the back of my hand.

"What??!", a perturbed Sherry responded, lifting the dryer off of her head while twisting her face at me.

"That's her", I whispered, using my eyes and forehead to point in Lisa's direction.

"That's who?", Sherry inquired a little to loud for my comfort.

"Shhh. That's Remington's wife.", I informed.

"That's her! Damn, you said she was cute and she *sure-in-the-hell* is. Wait a minute. I thought Remington was older. Did you tell me he was about 50-somethin'?", Sherry tried to gain understanding, as she'd never met Remington.

"46. But, that's not him with her.", I explained.

"Oh shit. See that's what I'm talkin' 'bout. Yo' ass was feelin' all bad and shit. And here she is with a nigga on the side herself!", Sherry spoke in confidence that made her voice a little louder.

"Shhhhh!", I tried to quiet her.

"If you don't stop *Shush-in'* me....", Sherry snapped without completing her threat.

I stared intently, watching Lisa and the mystery man's every interaction, while Lisa was unaware of my presence. Sherry's loud-talking threatened to blow my cover.

She is a model, he could be a male model she works with or a photographer, I gave her the benefit of the doubt in my mind.

My female instincts were that it probably wasn't true. But, I kinda hoped for it to be.

Apparently, Lisa was trying to get a walk-in appointment, which was the reason she was at the counter for so long. Once they squeezed her in, the 6'3, very handsome, model-like mystery man kissed her goodbye, full on the lips as Lisa angrily pushed him way, upset at his lack of discreetness as she scanned the room to see who'd seen it. The mystery man just laughed at her, pointed to his watch, most-likely clarifying a time that he'd pick her up.

Sherry was busy pinching my leg, trying to point-out what I'd already seen.

"I saw it Sherry, damn! Stop pinchin' my leg that shit hurts!", I grunted more disturbed that her painful pinching interrupted the thoughts that were going through my head than the actual pain itself.

When the beautician came to get me because my hair was dry enough for her to begin the styling process, Lisa first saw me. She had a look of fear on her face, as she tried to read my eyes to see if I recognized her. I gave no indication that I did. I just sat in the chair and discussed what I wanted to do with my hair with the beautician.

"Hey, Keisha. How you been doing", Lisa smiled at me as she glanced to see where I'd come from in an attempt to figure out whether or not I could've been present when the mystery man kissed her.

"That's my nickname.", I quickly lied in whisper over my shoulder to my beautician that had done my hair long-enough to know that wasn't my name.

Sherry was up-to-speed on the phony name Remington had me using. Though, her face almost gave it up until she remember.

"I'm doing good. How about you?", I said, realizing I shouldn't have asked because it kept the conversation going.

"Well, just trying to get ready for a modeling shoot. My photographer dropped me off to get ready for it.", she said giving much more information than would've been necessary from a non-guilty person.

"Hmmph." I heard Sherry grunt under her breath in the chair next to me.

I wanted to beat Sherry's ass for doing that. She was always good for saying or doing the wrong shit at the wrong time.

Lisa sat in the chair reading a magazine the whole time I was getting my hair styled. I'd witnessed her shaking her head to a beautician that came up to her.

» » » » » » » » » » » » » » » » « « « « « « « « « « « « « « «

Sherry was done before me. So she sat next to Lisa and skimmed through the current issue of *Essence Magazine* as she waited for me. When I was finally finished, paid the beautician and was making my way to exit, I waved goodbye to Lisa.

"Keisha. Can I talk to you a minute?", Lisa asked catching me and Sherry just outside the beauty salon doors.

"Sure. What's up?", I said.

"It's kinda personal.", Lisa said, looking at Sherry, indicating that she wanted to speak to me alone.

I turned to Sherry and quickly said, "I'll meet you in the car!", with a serious face and fast-enough before Sherry could get offended by Lisa's inference that she was an encumbrance. If I'd not done that fast, Sherry would've no doubt made one of her usual *off-the-cuff* remarks about Lisa cheating without thinking twice before blurting it out.

The beauty salon was in a strip-mall, so we walked down the sidewalk to a restaurant and sat in a booth near the window.

"I don't know if you saw the guy who dropped me off or not?", she said, pausing to give me a chance to verify whether I did or not.

She was trying to draw an answer, but I didn't give one. Instead, I just looked at her, close-mouthed, waiting for her to finish.

"Alright, look. We're sistaz and sistaz gotta stick together, right?", she advocated. "That guy is my man. I'm a baller-catcher and I think you're one too. I don't believe you're Remington's co-worker's niece. And I know your name ain't even Keisha – I could see it in your girlfriends eyes. Am I right?", she confided like we were the bank-robbers at our hideaway meeting place.

"Uhhhhhhh", I struggled to answer, not knowing which way to go because her comments were so unexpected. But I knew that if I didn't deny it in a quick manner that it would indicate that it must be true. Still I hesitated.

"Girl admit the shit. I know you've fucked Remington. I don't care. I just married the nigga for his money. I'm not gonna stay with him for the rest of my life. I'm just runnin' game just like you. You get what you want from him and I'll do the same. Let's just agree not to mess each other up, okay? Agreed?", Lisa said, removing all elements of her sophistication that I'd previously believed was her natural personality.

"Okay.", I said without actually admitting to my deeds or intent.

"And don't tell your nosy-girl in the car what we talked about. I can already tell that she's got a big mouth. It'll just fuck the both of us up", she said, genuinely placing her hand on top of mine.

"Okay.", I said again as though I were a foreign speaking immigrant that only knew that one word.

As Lisa got up to leave, she turned around and spoke.

"Oh, one more thing. What is your real name?", she tested the validity of the deal we'd just made by asking for honesty.

"Mysterious", I just answered.

Of course, the first thing I did when I got in the car was tell Sherry what Lisa and I had discussed after I watched Lisa re-enter the beauty salon.

Everyone was *playin'* everyone else. I was *playin'* Remington. Remington was *playin'* Lisa. And Lisa was *playin'* Remington. The only person that didn't know the whole deal was Remington. It was like one big Player-Merry-Go-'Round.

»»»»»»»»»»»»»»»»»»««««««««««««««««««

About a month later, Sherry had found what she called a new angle to get ballers. She'd begun to dance at *Smooth's* a hoodish Atlanta strip-club.

While it was true that ballers did go to strip-clubs, I thought it was her way to meet more of her *achilles heal ballers* – the thugs.

I tried to convince her not to, but she wouldn't listen, as usual. And I figured that I'd warned the girl enough in the past, so I wasn't going to drive myself crazy preaching the same old message.

Sherry actually enjoyed it. It gave her something to do during the daytime, as she worked the early shift from Noon to 8 PM. That was the one good thing about her decision. By working the early shift, she'd be gone by the time the club got rowdy and full of the really dangerous people.

I told her if she was gonna work at a strip-club that she should go to one that was more classy. Maybe a white one that's downtown or something. You know, catch some white-boy Inheritance-ballers looking for some black booty. But, I think part of the reason she didn't was 'cause she was tryin' to get her freak on too. And the hood-clubs provide the opportunity for her with both men and women. I did have to eat my words about not dancing at the strip-club when she hooked-up with a platinum-recording rap star she'd met in the VIP-room.

I didn't know that Sherry was really serious about the guy. He was right up her alley, but better than others in her past. Oh, he was thuggish for sure, but not hardcore. Well, maybe he was just ghetto. I guess, if she was gonna date a thug/ghetto baller it was better that he was an Entertainment-baller instead of a Street-baller.

He didn't even have any children, which I thought was unusual for a 24-year old black rapper. At first, I thought he was lying. Most of the rappers I knew had enough baby's mommas to count on at least two hands. Later I understood why he had no children when Sherry told me that he always wore a rubber, even while she was sucking his dick.

Sherry's ass was crazy about the boy and her baller-catching suffered while she was *dating* him. She thought I was jealous because she'd found someone, but I wasn't. Plus, he didn't nearly give her as much shit as other ballers. In my opinion, she was just *Dick-Whipped*, plain and simple.

One evening while they were dating, Sherry brought her crying self next door to my house. She was upset because he'd avoided her when she brought up the subject of marriage to him. I was just as shocked 'cause she'd never mentioned wanting to get married to me and I was her girl.

Out of pure desperation, Sherry attempted to trap him by getting pregnant. Whenever he was about to orgasm, he'd pull-off the condom so he could release his juices on her body. Sherry's stupid-ass had gone in the bathroom and scooped semen off her and inserted it into her vagina. It didn't work. And I was glad because we'd established rules about which ballers not to get pregnant by. At the top of the list were Entertainment Ballers. They look like a lot of money, but when their CD's are off the charts many actually owe the company. So, there'll be no fat child-support check.

Chapter Eight Whaaaat?!

Three weeks later, I was awaken by a loud banging on my front door. Whoever it was alternated between ringing the door bell and banging on the door.

Ding-dong-ding-dong, bang-bang-bang, ding-dong-ding-dong, bang-bang-bang was the irritating noise I heard.

"Who is it?!", I screamed back at the person on the other side of the door.

"Atlanta Police Department, mam. Open the door!", the stern voice responded.

I peeked through the peep-hole and saw three uniformed officers and a suit-dressed man with a badge clipped to his belt.

Cautiously I opened the door.

"Are you Mysterious Luva?", the suited-man said before I could get a chance to ask him what this was all about.

"Yes.", I admitted.

"We need to take you to the police station for questioning.", assertively he said.

"Police station? Questioning? About what?", I rambled in scared fashion.

"We're investigating the murder of Remington Charles. So, we need to ask you some questions about your relationship with Mr. Charles."

I couldn't believe what the detective said. Remington was dead.

I spent the next six hours down at the Atlanta Police Headquarters answering questions about my personal sexual relationship with Remington. I wasn't sure if they thought I killed him or not.

Remington's body was found in his car parked near Midtown Atlanta by Piedmont Park. He'd died from multiple gun shot wounds to the head and chest.

» » » » » » » » » » » » » » » » « « « « « « « « « « « « « « «

I don't know what I would've done without Sherry during this period of my life.

On my second visit to the station, when the police informed me of a $1.5 Million life insurance policy that Remington had taken out on himself after being promoted, Lisa immediately came to mind. Well, her and the mystery man.

I hesitated at first, but eventually dropped *dime* to the police that his Lisa was cheating on him and about the meeting that we had next door to the beauty salon.

The investigators wanted to set-up a meeting between me and Lisa in an attempt to gain more circumstantial evidence. She was already their prime suspect because she was the sole beneficiary of the life insurance policy.

Lisa had a rock-solid alibi, she was at home with the children during the time of the murders. So the police knew she'd not personally done the killings, but suspected that she'd hired someone.

Though they promised that they'd protect me if I cooperated, I wasn't sure how they could when I didn't even know who the mystery man was.

"You know, if you don't help us to bring them to justice, when the get-off, you know the first person they're gonna kill might be you. You're the only one who knows what Mrs. Charles was up to.", the detective attempted to scare me into compliance.

He did have a point. What would stop them?, I wondered to myself.

"But she doesn't even have my phone number, so she wouldn't know how to get a hold of me even if she wanted to meet with me", I explained the limited contact I'd actually had with Lisa to the police.

"But you did have her number, right?", the detective questioned.

"Yeah, but she knew I was sleeping with Remington for the money. If I called her, she'd be real suspicious!", I again tried to explain that we were not girlfriends or anything close to that.

Feeling like he'd at least gotten me to consider a possible sting operation because I was talking about the flaws in their plan, the detectives huddled outside the door of the interrogation room and held a private discussion.

"Okay Miss Luva, here's what we're gonna do. We get a surveillance warrant that will allow us to wire-tap Mrs. Charles' phone and to follow her around. We'll find a pattern of her movements and bring you with us so that it will appear as though you and Mrs. Charles' just happened to be at the same place at the same time. Is that okay with you?", he said with intense eyes.

"I don't know what you want me to do? Or what I'm suppose to get her to say?", I offered excuses.

I was nervous about saying yes, but at the same time, I didn't wanna shun the police department that promised to protect me. I was just confused and wished I'd never met Remington.

"Miss Luva, I know that you're concerned, but there's really nothing to be afraid of. We'll tell you what to say and do. Our officers will be there. You'll be *bumping* into Mrs. Charles' at a public location, lots of people. I promise you that. But we'll need to let the judge know that we have your cooperation along with your statement about Mrs. Charles' infidelity as grounds to obtain the surveillance warrant. Otherwise, we may not even be able to charge her with murder. She'll go free and we can't authorize protection for a non-cooperating witness. So, you'll be out there by yourself – all alone! So what do you say Miss Luva, will you help yourself by helping us?"

"Okay.", I agreed, feeling like I might end-up dead if I didn't.

»»»»»»»»»»»»»»»»»»«««««««««««««««««

The Atlanta Police Department had tracked Lisa's every move for two weeks. According to police, she'd even called my home phone on two occasions but left no messages.

The media attention on the suspicious murder of a high-ranking corporate executive was intense. It was all over the news. CNN, BET and all the national network news channels were covering it.

For my own safety, I was moved into protective custody at the Dunwoody-area Renaissance hotel, while the police awaited the right time to stage an *accidental* meeting.

It was driving me crazy to be confined in a hotel room day and night guarded by police officers. I couldn't talk to Sherry or my mother, who I'd not spoken to in several years. It didn't matter how nice the hotel was, I just wanted to get it over with, but the police were hoping to identify the mystery-man before arranging our *accidental* meeting. Unfortunately, Lisa had not been seen with any man during surveillance.

The police felt very strongly that she'd plotted the murders because the supposed grieving widow made strange moves after his death. First, she took the kids to their grandmothers and they remained there since their father's death. She hadn't made a single call to the children to check on how they were handling the situation. Secondly, she went on 6-hour casual shopping spree at Lenox Mall the day before the funeral. And finally, the day after the funeral, she'd contacted the insurance company attempting to collect the money. Not the normal moves of a woman writhing with sorrow, the police informed me.

During the two weeks after the murder, Lisa had grown tired of wrestling with the insurance underwriters. She wanted the money now. The insurance company stalled the dispersing of funds because the investigation of foul-play was not yet complete.

Shortly before the end of the third-week of protective custody, the police's patience paid off. Lisa had been recorded talking with a man. That talked in what was clear coded conversation and didn't stay on the phone for long.

The police played the tape for me hoping that I'd be able to confirm that it was the mystery-man. I'd told them that I really didn't hear his voice at the salon, but they played it for me, anyway.

They were able to trace the call to a cell phone number registered to a Demetrius Powell and within an hour of that conversation, police had obtained wire-tap and surveillance warrants for him.

Police quickly loaded me into a tinted window van parked in the parking ramp of the hotel. They escorted me into the van like Secret Service men did the President of the United States.

We drove to the home address of the man that Lisa had talked to and waited outside in the van for several hours hoping to get a glimpse of the man so that I could identify if he was the man I saw her with at the beauty salon.

He never did come out of the house and once darkness fell, we went back to the hotel. They wanted to make sure that I had a good view of the man during daylight hours. A 24-hour surveillance team was left behind to stay on top of him and they'd notify me at the hotel of any opportunities to view him.

Around 2 A.M., Demetrius Powell left his house and drove slowly by my house several times, circling the block again and again, the surveillance team had reported back in the middle of the night.

That news, scared the shit out of me. And I was worried about Sherry. Though I know they didn't know who she was or that she lived next door, but still I didn't want her to be in danger, even with the surveillance team watching his every move.

» » » » » » » » » » » » » » » » « « « « « « « « « « « « « « « «

My chance to identify Demetrius Powell as the mystery-man didn't come until late-afternoon the next day when he'd gone to work-out at *Tone-Rite* fitness gym in Stone Mountain. We sat outside the gym for over and hour waiting for him to exit.

"That's him. That's him.", I verified immediately upon seeing him leave the gym and walking towards his car in the parking lot.

"Are you sure? Look real close!", one of the detectives said to me in a hurried manner.

He instructed the other officer to slowly drive past the man, as I viewed him close-up through the tinted windows. The detective wanted to make sure that I'd gotten a good-enough look and make sure that I was 100% positive, knowing how long it took to even get this chance.

"I'm positive. That's the man that was kissing Lisa in the beauty salon. No question about it!", I reconfirmed.

» » » » » » » » » » » » » » » « « « « « « « « « « « « « «

Now that they'd identified who they believed was the actual shooter, the next step was for me to *accidentally* run into Lisa.

They wired my body with microphones. I was given instructions on what I needed Lisa to say on tape and how to go about getting the information.

The *accidental* meeting took place inside of a Starbucks coffee shop. Lisa immediately came up to me on sight. I'd told her that I was sorry to have heard about Remington and she brushed off my condolences to segue into whether or not the police had contacted me. As instructed by the police, I acted surprised by her comments and told her that they had not, which seemed to put her more at ease.

As we shared a table, I tried to get the information that the police wanted, but it was difficult bringing certain subjects up without sounding suspicious. Lisa turned around with each customer that walked in, the last one being a police officer that was in the van with me. He'd order a cup of coffee and sat near yet another police officer who'd come in before I did.

There presence did make me feel better, but I wasn't able to get her to be as candid as she'd been in the restaurant next to the beauty salon. And it turned out to be the last chance we'd have. Even without a confession, the Atlanta District Attorneys office proceed to execute a warrant for Lisa and Demetrius' arrest.

Chapter Nine A Time To End

Damn, the sun is hot today!, I thought to myself as I sat on a cot on the tropical Jamaican Island beach located in the back of my beach-front home while typing on my wireless *Dell* laptop computer.

The 6-week long trial was over. It'd taken 6-months to come before it came in front of a judge, most of which I spent secluded and police-protected in the south-Georgia town of Savannah.

After all I'd been through in the year, it was a shame that the case ended in a mistrial. Both, Lisa and Demetrius were freed due to a technicality.

Lisa was finally able to get the $1.5 Million from the life insurance policy. And because they were unable to be retried, the police thought I may not be in any danger. However, because the case was over, they could no longer provide on-going protection for me. That's what I get for cooperating without legal counsel. An attorney would've negotiated that even if my help didn't lead to a conviction.

It was the police's words "may not be in danger" that made me make the decision to leave the country. I had some money, but not enough to last my entire life in a different country.

I called a few of the ballers I'd known over the years for help. But after having given testimony in this case that was televised on *Court TV* and being characterized by legal reporters as a "no-good gold-digger", none of the ballers I'd knew returned my calls.

It was clear that my baller-catching career was over. I was retired.

I decided that Lisa shouldn't be the only one to become a millionaire from her baller-catching scheme. So, I'd come-up with my own plan that would take care of me for the rest of my life.

Remembering how interested the paparazzi were at every little detail of actor Kevin Jones' life, I decide to sell the sex-tape we'd made together and I'd stolen before returning to Atlanta from California.

When word got out that I was offering the tape to the highest bidder, Kevin even offered to buy it back for $500,000. Every offer he made, the paparazzi's reporting companies offered more. Finally, I ended-up selling it to an internet porn-company that featured many celebrity-sex video tapes. Tommy Lee & Pamela Anderson, Tonya Harding's Honeymoon, Paris Hilton's Wild Night, you name the celeb-sex video and they offered it for sale.

Amidst attempted legal injunctions filed by Kevin's attorney to prevent me from selling the tape, I finally completed the sale for a cool $2.3 Million! Although, I did have to spend $400,000 in legal fees and commissions to my attorney who'd actually brokered the deal.

I do miss the thrill of baller-catching a bit. Sometimes I do it for fun in Jamaica. But now, I'm the ballerette and I have to watch who I'm fucking.

My girl Sherry is still going strong in the game, even without me to be her in-person conscience. We do still stay in touch. She comes to Jamaica to see me and stays here about 10-days out of the month.

I spend a lot of my time writing, poetry mostly, except for this book.

While relaxing in the Jamaican sun, I'm working on my next novel entitled *Baller Catchers*, where I'll share all of my girl Sherry's *bizness*. Especially all the hot details of the stuff she's done right here in Jamaica. She doesn't know that I'm writing it yet, so if you know her, don't tell her – awight?

I don't need the money, but I do like sharing information about this baller-catching game.

As far as Sherry's *bizness* is concerned, I figure she shouldn't be so damn wild if she didn't want all of her shit shared.

And besides, I sold the tape, now why wouldn't I release Sherry's shit?

Now, Proceed To Catching A Baller 101 Section

CATCHING A BALLER! 101

The Instructional Guide

Everything You'll Ever Need To Know About Catching A Baller!

Catching A Baller Basics

1. Live In A Major Metropolitan City – It is virtually impossible to catch a baller in a small town. Though there are some real Smalltown Ballers, most are not. They are simply the most affluent big fish in the small pond.

My rule of thumb is simple. If your city doesn't have at least two major sports teams and a population of more than one-million people – Move! (*See Page-91 for Top-10 Cities To Catch A Baller List*)

2. Physical Fitness – Nothing turns-off a baller like fat! He can get that anywhere, even from his wife. You can't control how your face looks, but everyone can be in-shape! Get a membership to the health-club or a personal trainer. Work-out at least 2-3 times per week. Whenever you feel tired, just think about the other women you'll be competing with. Ask yourself whether or not you think they're at the gym right now? Then pack that duffle bag and do squats until you think your ass is gonna fall off. Let's keep it real. Sistaz got the ass. We invented the shit long before J.Lo! But contrary to popular belief, there is a such thing as too much ass. Stand in a mirror naked, with your butt facing the mirror. Squeeze your ass-cheek muscles. If you see dimples in your butt like it's a big black golf ball, you need to hit the gym – I don't give a damn how good you are at stuffing your ass into a pair of complimenting jeans!

3. Skin – Keeping your skin smooth and as blemish-free as possible is a must no matter what type of baller you're after. If you have re-occurring blemishes you may want to consult a dermatologist. Keep your skin moisturized at all times – no ash! Also, be careful of where you get tattoos. The more sophisticated baller may find tattoos a turn-off if they're located on your titties, belly-button area, arms, anywhere on your legs or high-up on the back of your shoulder. For the sophisticated baller, because they are professional, you may have to attend events with them. At the first sight of tattoos in these areas, they may have already decided they can't risk bringing you to a formal affair and introducing you to their boss. Other types of ballers may not care. However, I'd recommend not limiting the types of ballers you can go after.

4. Hair – Keep your hair as long as possible. 99% of ballers favor very long hair over short. The other 1% like medium-long hair. Get the point! Add hair if you need to. If you think you can get a baller with a *Florida Evans-from Good Times-short-fade-haircut*, you must be out of your damn mind! Stop listening to your girlfriends talking about how good your hair looks short! Do not go cheap on this!

5. Nails – Keep your hands soft and your nails well-manicured. French manicure is okay, but adding the ghetto fabulous designs on the tips will limit your option to the street baller types only. Do not forget about your feet. Make sure the nails look equally as good and your feet are baby soft.

6. Tattoos – They can be sexy and add to your look. But be careful not to limit yourself in the number of different types of ballers that you can go after. Tattoos in the wrong places on your body or of the wrong design will certainly do that. *For example*: A Corporate Executive Baller ain't gonna give you the time of day if you have a "tat" across your thigh that reads "Pooky". Tittie tattoos on cleavage areas are ghetto-fabulous. The best idea is to keep a tattoo well-hidden. You can always mention them to a baller. He'll be intrigued to one-day see it personally.

7. Piercing – Very stimulating to some ballers. The more sophisticated ballers may frown upon nose piercing or more than two-holes ear piercing. All ballers tend to love belly-button piercing. Clit and nipple piercing may pleasantly surprise the baller, even the more sophisticated ballers don't seem to mind these because they're hidden when you're on his arm at a social engagement.

8. Children– Just because you have children does not mean that you won't be able to catch a baller. However, the more children that you have does hinder your chances. If you do have children start setting-up a network of babysitters, so that you'll be able to accept a baller's invitations. Make sure to have at least two people that are solely for the purpose of last-minute babysitting. You don't want to get a surprise invitation to go to the Bahamas from a baller and you cannot accept it because you plane leaves tomorrow and your don't have a babysitter!

Defining A Real Baller

What's most sad is that a lot of women wouldn't know a real baller if they saw one! And I'm not talkin' about the suit-wearing, 1st Fridays-going, SUV-driving wanna-be-imitation-ballers.

If you happen to be one of these women who ain't gotta clue, let me break it down for you with a definition:

Baller: *adj. A real-baller is a man that can spend enough cash to make you rich without it hurting his lifestyle.*

Read this definition over and over again. This is Step-1 towards getting what you want. I believe it was Muhammad Ali who once said, *"You can't hit what you can't see!"*. The same is true for you. If you forget this definition of a baller or compromise it to make a man fit it, you'll never hit your target of gaining wealth.

There Are Many Different Types Of Ballers

Where many women make their first mistake is in failing to recognize that there are many different types of ballers. That's why they're unsuccessful in latching on to one. It takes savvy to understand what type of baller you're talking to and what his weakness is. Just about any decent looking woman can seduce a baller into sleeping with her, but can they seduce his wallet?

The first thing you gotta recognize is that ballers come in all shapes, sizes, ages and colors. Some have a Denzel-like smoothness about 'em. Other are like a refined-Urkel. Others may be older and married. No matter what the package looks like, they are all victims in my mind. They want to play this game. They need to play this game. It's up to you whether or not you're gonna let him play it better than you. It's very similar to a war or a chess game. The person who is best prepared normally wins. A big and basic part of that preparation is knowing the different types of ballers, their motivation and where to meet them.

These different types of ballers can be broken-down into nine categories: ***Business Owner, Corporate Executive, Athlete, Heir or Inheritance, Lotto, Street, Entertainment, Investment and Real Estate***.

Business Owner Baller - He normally owns more than one business, unless it's a huge revenue-generating business similar to a franchise restaurant like McDonalds.

I call these ballers *BOBs*. And not just for acronym purposes, but because they tend to actually have names that are main-stream like Bob, Bill, Jim or Mark. I don't know why that's the case. It's as though their parents were scared that if they gave him too ethnic of a name, he wouldn't be successful.

BOBs may be college educated with degrees in fields like finance, accounting and business. Usually he comes from two-parent households that live for and around his every successful venture. He may be biracial, or act as if he is. His speech tends to be proper and his jokes, corny. A majority of *BOBs* come from suburban neighborhoods. If he grew up in the inner-city, he most-likely was bused to a private school.

One hurdle or problem is that *BOBs* do have a thing for white girls or near-white girls (light-skinned black women). But don't give-up yet on *BOBs* because this obstacle is easily remedied.

If you're a dark-skinned black women, you can transcend these biases by speaking intellectually. Changing your mannerisms to that of a white girl (hair-flipping, high-pitched giggle, etc.) will work magic on him. He'll be confused and intrigued just like when you hear black people from England speak. They sound funny because it wasn't what you expected.

Main Weakness: Though they make a lot of money, *BOBs* are privately unhappy and somewhat insecure. They succeed more from the fear of letting proud family members down than they do from their true desire or love for the business they own. Also, they're not quite sure where they belong. Most of their time is spent with white people, battling stereotypes trying to prove that they're better than the "typical" black man.

Another weakness is their insecurity about sex. This is partially the reason they go after white women. They feel that there's less pressure to perform with white women, because most of the stringy-haired women they'd court would never have been near a big-dicked brotha that they'd not measure-up to. In a lot of cases, these *BOBs* are very wrong about their own dick size. It just goes to show how sheltered of a life they've been living. But, use it against them, anyway.

Love Making: *BOBs* make love. They are die-hard romantics that are searching for that woman that could gain mom's approval. At the same time, *BOBs* have a repressed freaky-side. But they're unable to find the key to unlock the door to their most-desired fantasies. A *BOB* will be overly conscious of pleasing you in bed. He'll look at your face during every stroke to see your reaction. Missionary style will dominate the sexual encounter, if not the entire encounter. You may get some decent oral from him, as he's probably gotten very good at it with the white girls. He will want you to return the favor by sucking on his dick, but won't risk asking. Instead, he'll gently attempt to maneuver your head to his dick. Hooking up with a *BOB* will ensure getting some of the best, gentle and tender sex.

Fake *BOBs*: Typically the 1st-Fridays going type. They have a nice car, maybe even own a home, but are still one paycheck away from poverty. They'll try to distract your attention with flamboyant-ness. Don't be fooled. Clues are all around. Keep your eyes open. If they take you to an expensive restaurant and pay with cash, they may not have a credit card. If he takes you to a theatrical play, look at the ticket stubs to see if they were complimentary from his company. Feel the fabric of his suit to see if it's made of expensive material. Get the picture?

Warning: Be careful not to fall in love with *BOB*s, which is very easy to do. They'll treat you like a queen – a wife-in-training. The love making will be a pleasurable break from the other types of ballers that you may encounter. Don't spend too much time around his relatives, because they'll want to adopt you as a member of the family, making it mentally difficult for you to run your games on him. Limit the amount of sex because your body could become addicted to it. The cuddling may feel nice, but remember, the money you can spend!

Good Places To Meet Business Owner Ballers: Usually at their place of business. Becoming a regular customer is a good way to opening the door to their heart. If they own something like a jewelry store, it may not be affordable to become a regular customer. In a case such as this, browse the store often, address him by first name and ask him to help you personally. Allow him to check you out, by steadfastly keeping your attention focused on the product that he's showing you. You may even *accidentally* (on-purpose) drop something on the floor, so that he can check your body out as you pick-up whatever it was that you dropped. Trust me, he'll be watching!

Corporate Executive Baller – Don't get this twisted. Here's where most women make their mistakes. This baller is not Middle-Management! Just *cuz* he where's a shirt-n-tie, has a secretary and owns a home don't make him a Corp-Baller. A real Corp-Baller has access to the company jet, makes upper 6-digits, closer to 7-digits than 5-digits, appears in his trade industry magazines and owns two or more luxury homes, maybe even a vacation home in a foreign country.

Corp-Ballers are very nice because they are extremely busy. They don't take up a lot of your time. However, they do want you to be accessible whenever they are in-town. Perks are abundant including lots of vacation trips and jewelry. They're constantly trying to please you because they don't have the time to spend with you, so they buy lots of gifts for no reason.

Many times the Corp-Baller is married, which is another plus. Even when you fall-out with a Corp-Baller, he'll spend years sending you hush-money. He can't afford to have his reputation tarnished in his business, not to mention having his trophy-wife suing the pants off of him!

The one down side is that getting cash from him can be a bit slow because his wife sees the bank statements too. The way he gets around this problem is by making ATM withdrawals in smaller amounts as though he's using the cash on his business trips. He'll most-likely charge most of your dates on his credit card and turn in receipts for reimbursement from his company as though it was a business meeting. It will also help him throw his wife off track because the cash that he's giving to you comes from withdrawals from their personal bank account under the pretense that the money was used on business trips and it will be reimbursed by the company. Without something to claim for reimbursement, so that he can actually get a reimbursement check, she'll become real suspicious. You never want your affair to come to the surface because your power is in the threat of it coming to the surface, not in it actually coming out. It's kinda like a criminal that's holding a gun to a hostages head. The police won't shoot, as long as the hostage is alive. If the gunman shoots the hostage, he'll be dead from bullets 3-seconds later.

Main Weakness: A lot of Corp-Ballers are married. They're constantly worried about getting caught cheating. Gradually step-up on the things you want from him. Hint at that you're getting tired of "sneaking" around with him. He'll believe that you want to bring y'alls relationship out in the open for everyone to see. That'll scare the shit out of him. So, he'll appease you by giving in to your material wants!

Love Making: Some Corp-Ballers do actually make love to you. Others want a break from their normally tame sex routine with their wife. So, they expect a little more spice from you. Send him home smiling every time. The more often you do this, the more he'll be wondering why he's in the relationship with his wife.

Fake Corp-Ballers: Just like the Fake Business Owner Ballers, the Fake Corp-Ballers tend to be the 1st-Fridays going type. Real Corp-Ballers are far to busy for a pseudo networking party. They attend real ones on the golf course, luxury resorts and industry parties at lavishly decorated locations. A big clue that you may be talking to a Fake Corp-Baller is when he tells you too much about who he is in the first 5-minutes. Don't get me wrong, the Real Corp-Baller does have a huge-ego and will brag to you, but not right away. Other clues are, if you are able to call him at work without going through two executive secretaries, then he's probably not as high-up in the company as he's claiming to you.

Warning: Corp-Ballers tend to work themselves into the ground. Many burn-out. You don't want to be around when this happens. Everything will go-to-hell all at the same time. Problems at work, with his wife and possibly some financial issues will make him very volatile. Read the signals of him not returning you calls as fast as in the past, complaints about money that you're asking for from him and complaints about his company. Though they are sophisticated, you have to understand they've spent the better part of their life being defined by the authority they carry in the company, when that's in jeopardy or gone completely, it is possible that he could flip out! Just think about all the stock-brokers who committed suicide after the 1987 Stock-Market Crash and those that entered their company's building wielding a gun. Get away fast at the first sign of his decline, you don't want him blaming you!

Good Places To Meet Corporate Executive Ballers: Lounges or bars of an upscale hotels like the Ritz-Carlton, Fortune 500 Companies Industry Trade Conventions (they're easy to spot – they're the guys every one is surrounding laughing at all their jokes). Expensive men's clothing stores that carry suits like Armani.

Athlete Baller – This is the most common baller that comes to a woman's mind. And, it's where the term originated, referring to the basketball players as "ballers".

The Athlete Baller is one of the best ballers to catch. They'll pay your rent, buy you a car, give you plenty of cash. But, don't ever think that you'll be his only woman! You won't.

Marrying a Athlete Baller is very profitable, though it may be difficult. Having a baby by one will keep you paid for life, although you'll have a child to raise for 18-years. Marrying is the best option. You may even seduce an 18-year old star, early in his college career, so that he'll view you as not a groupie later when he goes pro.

Main Weakness: Their egos are so huge, it can be used as a weapon against them. When they're playing poorly they need someone to say that they love 'em anyway. Let that be you. Also, they take risks and defy odds so often as a part of their job that it trickles into their lives off the court. Condoms are rarely used. So, if you're looking to get pregnant, that shouldn't be too hard.

Love Making: Make no mistake about it, Athlete Ballers are buck-wild! They don't make love until they actually fall in love. Further more, they tend to be huge guys in body-size and dick-size. They will try to get you to be a part of a harem – sleeping with 2 or more women on the same night at the same time. They will attempt to get you and the other woman to sex each other. They will want to fill every one of your orifices, so be prepared.

Fake Athlete-Ballers: It's easier to spot the Fake Athlete Baller than any of the other types of Fake Ballers. But, some of them have become creative. You'll see former college athletes, who you might even recognize, that didn't make it to the big leagues, or was cut early in the season. They'll tell you that they're injured and that's why they're not listed on the roster. They do have more money than the Average Joe, but you're after a baller, right? Sometimes you can use these *Could've-Would've-Should've-Been* Fake Ballers to get to the real ones. They're still friends with the real ones and respected by them. They'll be able to get you to the private room parties where you can try for their boyz.

Warning: Be careful of the Athlete Baller's dick-size. They can, and if you let 'em, will put a hurtin' on your ass in bed. Also, they sleep around a lot. Sexually transmitted diseases must be in the forefront of your mind! Baby-mama-drama is also likely, especially with Athlete Ballers over the age of 25.

Good Places To Meet Athlete Ballers: Nightclubs, strip-clubs and major entertainment events like Concerts or Record-Release Parties and After-Parties. Athletes are lime-light hogs. They live for people coming up to them and telling them how much they love them. Also, hotel lobbies when they're staying out-of-town. After practice at their sports training facility. However, the training facility is well-guarded to keep women out. But, it's been done before, you just have to be creative in how you're gonna get in.

Heir or Inheritance Baller – Normally white or foreign guys whose parents were extremely wealthy and he has nothing better to do but look for all the love that his parents didn't give him while they were hard at work making the millions of dollars that's now his. Though, don't be surprised if you find several black inheritance ballers. There's a great number of Foreign Country Inheritance Ballers (Middle-Eastern, Asian, African, etc.) that are available. The most major hurdle is cultural practices and their family's non-acceptance of you. But, the world is changing and they are interested in dating outside their race.

Main Weakness: They're not use to dealing with sistaz. When there's an issue pull-out your best sistah-girl style on his ass and watch him back-peddle and give-in to your every request. Tone it down a little with the Foreign Inheritance Baller 'cause he'll be turned-off completely and decide that it's just easier to go back to dating females from the same ethnic origin.

Love Making: The sex can be a little strange venturing into the nasty. The idea of butt-licking will make you wanna say "yuk", until he's performing it on you and your eyes are crossed and your mind is thinking, *"Damn, I never knew that would feel that damn good!"*. Try not to get hooked on it. But shit, that's like telling someone to use Crack-Cocaine in moderation. Yo' ass, no pun intended, is gonna be hooked. Just don't perform it on him. The best you give him is a moistened finger or two circling his A-hole, but that's it! Unless you just wanna put your fingers in his ass just to see him moanin' like a bitch.

Fake Heir or Inheritance Ballers: Generally there aren't too many fake ones. Though you will find those who will attempt to dazzle you with who their parents or relatives are and what they do. If the relative their associating themselves to is in a career that's job-oriented, I don't care how nice the title sounds, they're not an Inheritance Baller. But, if it's a company their parents own, then investigate more.

Warning: Be careful to not let him turn you into his "Black-Girl Booty" phase, where he's satisfied his curiosity of sleeping with a big-butt black woman and now wants to go back to the world where he's accepted.

Good Places To Meet Heir or Inheritance Ballers: There's not a general location where you can meet these type of ballers. You just kinda run into them anywhere. I mean, it ain't like they got a "Inheritance Baller Bar" or something. For the foreign ones, dining at restaurants that serve the native dishes is a good way to meet them.

Lotto Baller – The least common of the ballers. This would be some guy who was finally lucky enough to actually hit the lottery after years of spending most of his paycheck trying. He's going to be short-lived for the baller-catcher because most of his money will be spent in just a few years. There'll be lotsa competition for the money and his family will tell him that you're no-good for him. Meanwhile, they'll be trying to drain him for every penny on get-rich schemes with not-so-subtle implications that he's forgotten about his peoples. But the good thing is you can get a lot of money in a short period of time. Especially if you catch him just after he's won the money!

Main Weakness: New to the money and anxious to feel like a baller. Very free with the cash, especially early after winning it. Looking for the cute women that he'd been unable to get before he won the money.

Love Making: Anywhere from love-making to wild bondage sex. Depending on age and what he's looking for. Don't push him too far away from what he wants. If he wants to make love, don't turn it into wild adventurous sex.

Fake Lotto Ballers: There are really no Fake Lotto Ballers.

Warning: The money will go very fast. So get your share and be gone. Never marry a Lotto Baller. Although you share the money, you'll also get half of the debt he'll be sure to be acquiring and you may not be able to get out fast enough.

Good Places To Meet Lotto Ballers: Watching the news of where a Lotto Baller lives or where he bought the winning ticket will give you a clue as to what local bar to hang-out in. He will be in that bar soon to hear the *hoopin'-n-hollarin'* from neighborhood buddies and to buy the bar a round of drinks.

Street Baller – Most commonly drug-dealers or a person associated with some sort of illegal activity. It might be some type of scam the baller has worked-out that's probably highly-unethical bordering on the illegal and may one-day come to the determination of a judge.

Street Ballers can be pimps as well. You'll have to make sure that he knows that you ain't a candidate for his pimpin' games. You're the one who's gonna be his main-girl –well, so he thinks.

Main Weakness: Street Ballers love to shine. If you got that One-In-A-Million type of look and body, he'll bend over backwards for you despite there being a bunch of decent women trying for him.

Also, because of their occupations, they're in constant need of places to hide or "wash" their money to avoid the IRS, law enforcement or theft. They need someone they feel they can trust and that might be you. Don't do anything stupid like money-laundering. However, he may want you to hold on to tens of thousands of dollars while he goes out of town. If he goes to jail during that trip you could be sitting pretty with a lot of money. But I'd still suggest that you leave town even if he's sent to the *pen* for life.

Love Making: Street Ballers tend to come from hard lives and rough streets. Their sex is a mirror of their lives – hard. They're gone try to beat-up the pussy and do the unthinkable with you. Anal is as likely as the sun rising tomorrow. A threesome at some point is a given. Just make sure that you out-work the other girl. Or, if he has you and the other women doin' each other, make sure you make that bitch look like a teenager by having her cummin', kickin' and beggin'—ASAP! He'll know that you're the real deal and not her.

Fake Street Ballers: I guess I wouldn't call 'em Fake Street Ballers as much as not as successful in the game yet as they're portraying themselves to you. More like ballers-in-training. Their cars are not as tight and their wads of cash not as phat. But, that may change in the blink of an eye.

Warning: Danger is always nearby just by the nature of their professions. Rough sex and insults will be common place. I'd advise you to get-in and get-out as fast as possible.

Good Places To Meet Business Owner Ballers: Where-else? – Da Streets! Truthfully, that's not the only place. Working at a strip-club you'll have your pick of them. Be careful though, do not to date Street Ballers from rival gangs. You'll be the first they'll kill. In fact, forget the gang member baller completely! It ain't worth it.

Entertainment Baller – This is a vast range of ballers. Record-Producers, Recording Artists, Agents, Lawyers, Television Actors, Writers, Magazine Publishers, Movie Producers, Promoters, Top-Level Photographers and more fall into this category.

Main Weakness: They are extremely busy with their schedules, appearances and editorial deadlines that they don't have time to read the signs that you're running a game on them.

Love Making: *E-Ballers* love making has a wide range from the extremely freaky to those whose business life is freaky enough for them that they want simplistic love making. You'll have to read which one you have on your hands. Let him take control—that'll be your clue.

Fake Entertainment Baller: There are a lot of these! Everyone's a photographer, model scout, film-maker, record-producer or a soon-to-be platinum recording artist.

Warning: Do not get pregnant by the E-Baller! While the money flows freely now, you have to understand that they could have a net-worth of zero. Or worse yet, they may actually owe the record company money. E-Ballers fall-off quickly into obscurity when the game changes. Getting tied to an E-Baller by bearing his child could lead to some serious dangers, especially when he's no longer popular. He'll cling to the baby, looking to put meaning back into his wilted life.

Good Places To Meet Entertainment Ballers: 40% of the ballers are found in New York or Los Angeles. But don't pack your bags yet, there's still 60% spread throughout the rest of the country. Many of the Entertainment Ballers reside in their home states to avoid the rat-race atmosphere. Just think about all the major players in the music industry that have their studios in places other than New York or L.A. – Jermaine Dupri (So So Def -Atlanta) and Master P (No Limit Records – New Orleans), just to name two. A lot of the actual music stars also do not live in New York & Los Angeles.

Investment Baller - This baller is normally not a Financial Planner, although he could be, if he's doing financial planning for other ballers. But for the most part, he'll work for a large firm or brokerage house that has commercials on television. Most of them are actually stock-brokers, not planners. Look at his business card to see his job title. If the word "planner" appears, he's most-likely not a baller.

Investment ballers are definitely the most debonair of the baller types. Always dressed finely in designer suits and shirts starched so sharp they could cut. The older ones have a touch of gray hair delightfully placed in their side-burns. And their speech is so invigorating that you could listen to them all day. They're always so positive in demeanor; they'll make you feel as though anything is possible.

Not as many as you might think are actually married. Some were just too busy to actually settle down, while others may have been divorced for 10-years or more.

Investment Ballers are nice because you can actually learn from them. And they make for good relationships. Now, don't think I'm going soft on them. You're still gonna run your game on them, too. All that I'm saying is that you can enjoy the time you spend with them as well.

Main Weakness: Part of their ability to succeed relies greatly upon them being able to spot trends, so they're very analytical. Skepticism is a way of life for them. However, they're all dying to find something they can believe in. A place where they can relax, turn off their brains and just chill. No matter the cost!

Love Making: Investment Ballers tend to be love-makers. Not as freaky as the others, but very experienced. You'll be surprised how well they can make you orgasms with the most simple routine movements. They won't need a lot of time to learn your body's best spots, that's how seasoned they are!

Fake Investment Ballers: Normally Financial Planners that have just completed their company's licensing program. They're in such a hurry to tell you what they learned it will drive you nuts.

Warning: Don't invest with them. You don't want your money tied to a relationship. I don't care how much they want to help with your future, invest your money with an Investment Baller that you ain't fuckin'!

Good Places To Meet Investment Ballers: Usually financial seminars. They're relatively cheap to attend, normally about $60-$100. Or, hang out at upscale bars located near the financial district around happy hour time.

Real Estate Baller – I ain't talking about a real estate agent selling normal residential houses. A Real Estate Baller is one that may sell property, but it's land is for major corporation development, million-dollar homes, luxury office developments or he owns the development corporation.

Main Weakness: They're so consumed with turning a profit on property, they're somewhat out of touch with regular human emotions. They can easily be made uneasy with excessive overt flirting. They don't know exactly how to handle it because they're used to rules the have a good grasp on. Keep them guessing!

Love Making: Real Estate Ballers are quirky, not really freaky, but still weird. They want you to say things during sex that ain't normal like call them by a different name so they don't feel like they're cheating on their wife. They also like to play childish sex games, instead of getting right to the action. May even spend money on elaborate costuming that's just gonna end-up on the damn floor anyway.

Fake Real Estate Ballers: Regular residential real estate brokers. They'll talk about projects like it's their own.

Warning: Just like with Investment Ballers, never put your money into their investment. In some cases, Real Estate Ballers are making shady deals and using tactics that are unethical and maybe illegal. But, that's how they make their money that you're gonna take from them.

Good Places To Meet Real Estate Ballers: City, County or State council public board meetings. You've seen them before while flipping through your cable channels on your way to watching HBOs *Sex In The City*. It's those meetings with the city officials sitting behind ugly fake-wood benches with name plates in front of them, talking about provisions and variances and shit like that. I know, it's boring as hell, but don't let how the men dress at the meeting fool you. They are some super-rich SOBs dressing down to look ordinary so they can get the city to subsidize land they plan to develop with a 10-million dollar building.

Understanding The Baller Mentality

As varied as there are types of ballers that you've just seen, so to should your approach be to each of them.

Not knowing or understanding a baller's motivation is about as good as making collard-greens without the salt-pork. You ain't gonna have no flava to your game.

Tendencies of Ballers

Ballers feel entitled, plain and simple. Most of them feel because of their money, they can have anything they want. And for the most part, it's true. Women who would ordinarily pass them by are now flocking around them.

Ballers are secretly insecure. Some ballers were nerds that have found popularity through wealth, but they know that's the reason. Even the athlete or entertainment ballers that have been popular their entire existence have become so dependent on such attention, they're lost when they don't get it.

Ballers are about making money. Money is the key to their status in the public, which is the key to their lifestyle, which is the key to their social lives.

Ballers are very confident. Even times bordering on the side of arrogant. They've faced many challenges previously and usually come-out victorious. Do not let arrogance scare you away.

Becoming A Baller Magnet

Learning how to attract ballers is the key to success. You must have some uniqueness about you. Some women have it physically. They may have an exotic look: slanted eyes, naturally wavy hair, exotic skin tone color or brickhouse body. Some have it in the form of their body shape. Some have it in their demeanor or style.

Equally as important to being a baller-magnet is knowing where the ballers are. Ballers don't find you, they just think they do.

There are a variety of places you should go, depending on the type of baller you're trying to attract ranging from club scenes to county government meetings. Read the baller descriptions on previous pages to refresh yourself on where you should spend your time. Also, later in this book you'll find a list of Top-10 Cities for baller-catching.

At social settings, never stand alone. Some may think that if you're alone a baller will feel free to come talk to you, right? Wrong!! If you're alone, he'll think that you're not popular, don't belong or that your husband is in the bathroom.

Instead, bring an overweight, unattractive or married friend to the engagement. Talk with other women until you've created a posse of women. People are attracted to crowds and men are especially attracted to crowds of women. While the other women are busy yapping about duvets and the latest episode of *Soul Food*, you'll be discreetly glancing the room for potential ballers.

Once you've spotted one and have caught his eye, act as though you're ashamed that he caught you looking by quickly turning your body back into the group. Count to about 12, then peek over your shoulder to see if he's still looking – he is. Dart your head once again into the group's conversation. This time, count to about 20 and then excuse yourself from the group and walk towards the ladies room. Should a friend want to go with you, decline or let her go alone. Don't worry about the baller going after her. He won't. He feels as though he already has a connection with you.

As you're walking to the ladies room, the baller will pounce on the opportunity, as he thinks he's caught you peeking twice. When he tries to speak to you, be polite yet confident and let him know that you're headed to the ladies room. Don't give him a chance to say much. He'll be confused because he was sure that you were going to be excited to have him talking to you and now it seemed as though you brushed him off. Walk about 6-to-8 steps away from him, turn around and say, "I'll be back in a minute". His ass'll be waiting for you like a puppy at feeding time. A sense of renewed hope will fill his mind, as he prepares his best conversation while you're in the ladies room. Don't spend more than 8-minutes in the restroom. Upon exiting, try not to look as though you're wondering if he's there or not. Chances are he will be. Even if he's not, he's just around the corner. However, do not go to him. Instead, walk as though you're heading back to the group. He'll wanna catch you before you get back there.

You may use this technique several times, even in the same night with the other baller watching. Though the other baller will see another baller talking to you, it'll do nothing but make him want you that much more because he views you as being the desired-by-all woman!

Believe it or not, another way to meet other ballers is through one that you're dating. It's true! Most ballers are risk-takers and even though he says he's this guy's boy, he'll sleep with you on the side.

TOP-10 Cities To Catch A Baller!

#1 – Atlanta

Don't be scurrd to travel or move to the ATL. Atlanta is the Black Baller Mecca of the south. Many entertainers, athletes and other rich men choose to reside in Atlanta because of its warm climate, southern hospitality and outstanding social scenes. Competition is stiff among baller-catchers, but the good thing is that there are plenty to catch! Also, Atlanta is a great place to catch a star on the rise, before they become world-wide famous! For the big-booty ladies, the ATL is definitely the place for you.

#2 - Las Vegas

Land of the High-Rollers! This is a good vacation destination where you might catch a baller. Flowing drinks will allow you to grab quick cash. Don't ignore the white-boy ballers looking for a little taboo black-booty, I mean, black-beauty on their trip away from their white-world back in Wisconsin or where-ever they're from. They'll tell you that you look like Janet Jackson, Serena Williams or any star that's known for their butt. Get classy-hip-hop on their ass and you'll leave with the trip paid for and more!

#3 - New Orleans

Nawlins is another good vacation spot, especially during Mardi Gras. Rich college boys looking for fun with their pockets filled with cash and daddy's credit card.

Looking for the more mature black ballers? Check out N.O. during the Essence Music Festival or their many Jazz Festivals. The range of baller choices is huge, from upscale middle-aged men to the Athletes & Music Stars.

#4 – Dallas

Are you surprised about Dallas? Don't sleep-on Big D! The "D" in Dallas stands for development. Dallas is perpetually growing everyday. Where there's economic growth, you'll be sure to find a range of ballers associated with it!

#5 - Los Angeles

L.A. is no surprise, I'm sure. Movie stars, entertainers and those associated with the entertainment industry from producers, attorneys, investment brokers make L.A. a beautiful place for baller-catchers. To be successful in L.A. you'll have to lose some of your bias about race, cultures or what a baller looks like. There are plenty of big-time ballers you may pass-by if you're not careful! Date 'em all! Out there, ballers have more freedom and are not pressured by typical U.S. societal pressures.

#6 – Chicago

Chicago is like an old pair of shoes, you just can't bring yourself to throwing them away because they feel too damn good. Chi-Town is one of the most fun cities to catch a baller because of its old-world charm. Ballers from the Windy-City love it there and enjoy your visits, despite the fact that you're costing them bundles of money each time. You'll have the most fascinating dates with ballers that'll take you to the most unlikely spots featuring the best entertainers. More than the baller, the nightlife of the city will seduce you.

#7 - New York

Obviously New York has tons of ballers. This is a place only for the most experienced baller-catcher. The NYC ballers are very seasoned and will be able to spot an amateur baller-catcher's game from a mile away. They'll have you thinking that your game is working well and the next thing you'll know, he'll have you trickin' for money to pay your rent.

#8 - Washington DC

America's capitol offers many opportunities to seduce Corporate-Ballers who are often in-town lobbying lawmakers. Stay away from the lawmakers, judges and senators themselves! That's a whole different level. Very serious. You don't wanna be caught in that world. Chocolate-City is excellent for both the Classy Baller-Catcher and the Ghetto-Fab Baller-Catcher.

#9 – Miami

International cities always present great opportunities to diversify you baller portfolio. This is very true in Miami. Young ballers, older retired ballers, foreign ballers, entertainment ballers, business owner ballers (with businesses in the tourism industry) and more are found in this fun baller playground of a town. Not a bad idea to learn a little Spanish.

#10 – Houston

What's happening with Houston is similar to what occurred to Atlanta in the 1980's. Upwardly mobile ballers are choosing to live in Houston for climate and other reasons. Companies are selecting to base their headquarters there as well, thereby changing the economics in the city.

Honorable Mention Cities: Detroit, Phoenix, Boston, Minneapolis, Philadelphia and Charlotte.

How To Talk To A Baller

Being able to speak a baller's language is important. There's not just one language but many. Learn a little about the industry of the baller you're trying to catch. Industry terms and principles. You do not have to be an expert, just don't be an idiot. With the exception of the Entertainment Baller, nothing turns a baller off or clues him in faster to your intent than you not knowing anything about his career-field. It will be very clear that your being at an event was not coincidental it was a devised plan to get his money.

Setting The Trap

Know What You're Working With!

Make sure that your opinion of yourself is not inflated. On the other hand, do not sell yourself short.

Too often I hear women whose opinions of themselves are way out of sync with reality. Light-skinned women who think they're *All-That* just because of their complexion and they're actually ugly! Women with brickhouse bodies talking about how their hips are too big! Sexy-petite divas that wished they had more body! Big-tittied females thinking they're *Jet Beauty* material and they ain't got no ass at all!

Ballers WILL take advantage of this phony thinking or insecurity. They'll break your ass down until they have you right where they want you.

The toughest thing for a woman to do is truthfully critique her own body. But, in this game there's no room for lying to you.

Stretch Marks – Never a good thing. There are all types of creams on the market to help reduce, fade and remove stretch marks. There's no excuse to have them.

Breasts – There are basically three things guys use to evaluate your breasts: Breast Size, Firmness and Nipple Quality. To be a baller-catcher at all, you must have a minimum of 2 out of these 3 things in your favor.

Breast Size – Don't worry too much about size, unless all that makes-up your titties are the nipples, or if you're an A-Cup. B-Cups are good, especially if it's a Full-B. C-Cups are real head-turners. More than a Full-C may be a problem that may have to be rectified with breast-reduction surgery. The only exception is if you're such a damn brickhouse that you got an ass to match that D-Cup, which is very rare! With those big melons, you'll look very top-heavy. Remember the focus is still your butt. Nice size titties are a bonus for the baller.

Firmness – Saggy or non-firm breasts are not attractive to ballers. To test to see whether your breasts are too saggy for a baller, place a pencil under the base of your breasts. If the pencil doesn't fall to the ground, your breasts are actually resting on your upper torso (stomach) instead of self-supporting as they once were. Saggy breasted wanting to become baller-catchers should seriously consider getting a breast-lift.

Firmness is not just about whether your breast pass the pencil-test. Your breast could pass the test and still have a mushy-ness about them. Breast-tissue comes in many forms. The more dense the breast tissue, the more firm the breast will feel to the baller. Fortunately there are several products on the market to help with breast tissue density like *Bloussant*. It comes in pill-form and will help you regain the way your breast felt when you were first developing them and increase fullness. Like everything in life, it does cost money, but it's well worth it.

Nipples – Ballers love suckable nipples. There's really nothing you can do about the type of nipples you have. But it is important to know when you do have the kind of nipples that ballers love. If your nipples are long and narrow like a straw, you've got the shit! Ballers can't wait to flick them with their tongue. Erect nipples that stand-out close to a ½-inch or longer are ideal to ballers. If you have 1-inch erect nipples, you'll have a hard time prying a baller's lips off of your titties. He'll wanna stay there all night!

Also, visually, ballers prefer the ring around the nipple (areola) to be smaller in diameter. Normally no more than 1 ½ to 2 times the size of the diameter of the actual nipple. If you've had a baby and breast-fed, this may have expanded the diameter of the ring around your nipple. Use coco or shay butter around the outer ring (areola) to try to reduce the diameter.

Butt – There are all different types of butts. Pear-shaped ones, round like a bowling ball ones, high-riding ones, low riding ones, narrow but still cute ones – the list is endless.

Legs – Skinny legs are the worst thing you could have. If you're a woman with a petite frame and have been unable to gain weight in your legs, here's a suggestion: You may have to eat more starchy food, risking gaining weight in other areas. You'll just have to work-out that much more. At the gym, focus on making your legs more muscular by using weights. Consult your personal trainer, he'll tell you what you should do. Building more muscle-tone gives you an exception in a baller's eye. He'll just think that your legs are smaller because you work-out often.

On-the-other-hand, thick legs are good, but some women take this a little too far. Cellulite and loose-shaking skin is not sexy! And don't think that a baller can't tell, just because you've stuffed your over-thickness into some designer jeans.

Juicy-plump, yet athletic legs is what your goal should be. You'd only need to turn-on the television to get your examples in Serena Williams and Beyoncè Knowles. That's what's hot right now.

Weight – This is where most women make the mistake of cheating themselves right out of the baller-catching game. The key word in brickhouse is "brick" not "fat". It won't matter that you got an incredible ass that measures 51" around and a 38-C bra size, if your waist is 36"! You just have the shell of a brickhouse that's swollen into a fat-house.

I can't say this enough – Your waist is the key to a sexy shape. Your waist, not your breast. Your waist, not even your butt. Your waist!! Women with smaller butts and a tiny waist appear more curvy because of the contrast between their hips and waist. The point is your waist! Get it?

Losing weight around your middle is about the toughest area to get in shape. It requires using muscles women don't enjoy using. Crunches and side sit-ups are necessary routines. But, there's nothing sexier to ballers than a women with tight abs. Running or fast-jogging will help reduce over-all body fat and speed-up your metabolism, making it easier for you to see the benefits of your sit-ups faster.

On the next page you'll see how you can tell if you're at the right weight for the ballers. This formula calculates the Maximum Weight for Baller-Catchers.

The Ideal Weight For Baller-Catchers Formula

________	**Your Height (inches)**
________	**x PPI Ratio (pounds per inch)**
________	**= Your Ideal Weight For Ballers**

*** Add 4-lbs. for C-Cup Bra Size; 6-lbs. for D-Cup; 5-lbs. for Medium Butt Size and 7-lbs. for Large Butt/Legs***

PPI Ratio Chart	
Your Height	Your PPI Ratio
5'0 to 5'4	1.91
5'5 to 5'7	2.03
5'8 & Taller	2.20

Here's an Example:

The Subject: A 5'6" Women (66-inches tall) with a C-Cup bra size and a large butt

Formula

66 inches x 2.03 PPI (pounds per inch) = 133.98-pounds + 4-lbs(C-Cup) + 7-lbs. (Large Butt) = **144.98-Pounds is her Maximum Weight**

Taking Care Of Your Body!

Besides working-out to stay in shape, there are many things that should be done to take care of your body.

Manicures and pedicures should be done regularly. There's no excuse for crusty feet in this game.

Skin care is very important. Your skin should glow. If you have pimples, blemishes or other skin problems, see a dermatologist. It's a worthwhile investment that you're making in yourself.

Now, with that said, it's time to move on to the games to run on a baller as a part of setting the trap.

Games To Run On A Ballers

Shock-N-Surprise Game

This is when you do something that is far from the image you've created. For the laid-back ***Business Owner Baller***, you might invite him over to watch a movie, except it's a porn movie! Or maybe just invite him over and have a collection of porn tapes or nude magazines sitting out in plain view as you go to the kitchen.

He'll be amazed and impressed by your assertiveness and confidence. At the same time, you'll be striking a chord in his inhibited sexual mind.

Challenge His Manhood Game

Challenging a baller's manhood is maneuvering yourself in a position of strength. You can challenge a baller's manhood in two ways – Sexually & Financially.

As I'll explain later on in more detail, it is important to have the upper-hand in bed with a baller. This will allow you to challenge him sexually. By using some of my techniques that'll make him orgasm quickly, you can play the disappointed role, which will be a great blow to his ego. However, be careful not to be so convincing that he doesn't want to further embarrass himself and chooses to never see you again. Show disappointment and then be understanding.

All ballers fall for this game. Most have an over-inflated view of themselves sexually just waiting for you to crush it. Once that view has been properly crushed and slowly pieced back together by you, you can get anything you want from a baller. He'll actually be eager to do it because he views you as someone that he can be less than perfect in front of without it getting around.

Challenging a baller financially is a much more delicate approach. Using words like "it's only…" when you're out shopping with him is the best way. Also, comparing purchases made for you from previous guys (real guys or ones you invent) will also strike a chord in a baller's financial manhood. No self-respecting baller likes to be 2nd-place in anything or to anyone!

Keep Yourself New Game

As a part of keeping a baller interested, you must continuously re-invent yourself. He's gotta feel that if he lets you go now, he'll be missing something new just around the corner.

Show him things that he didn't know right away like that you know how to play the piano, or that you can sing or that you speak a foreign language.

After you've gone out a couple of times. Do not move at his every beck and call. Sometimes make yourself too busy. Talk about events that you've gone to during the time you've known him when he wasn't present. He'll wonder if you're seeing someone else and wanna step-up his game to get an exclusive on you.

The Jealousy Game

Ballers feel superior to everyone. *"How dare anyone compete with me, don't they know who I am?"* is how a baller thinks.

Making a baller compete for you is a bait your baller-fish will be sure to take. They'll wanna prove to themselves that they're the winner.

When you meet a baller, always say that you're in a relationship with someone, but don't sound like you're too enthused about it. He'll be sure to want to prove that he's better for you and show you what he's made of financially.

I'm Bored Game

When you find that is your baller is trying to slip you into a relationship that predicated on sharing quality time rather than spending money, it's up to you to make him aware that you're becoming bored. This will wear on him a bit.

When you go out to dinner, shopping or take vacations, show him an extreme change in your demeanor. This is a subtle way for him to pick-up on how to keep you happy, rather than blurting out "I want some more money!"

Making Bets Game

Ballers are very competitive and often enjoy wagering on just about anything. Chances are you've witnessed the baller doing it with his boys.

Make bets with him. Choose expensive items, jewelry, etc. as prizes should you win the bet. This is like stealing because if you lose he's not gonna make you pay, he just wanted to prove that he's "da man". But if you win, you'll get your prize.

Makin' Love Game

When it comes time to sex a baller, your goal is to get him to make love to you rather than just fucking you. You want him to be sensual and in the face-to-face positions. It may seem silly, but it will cause him to have a more personal connection and increase the chance of him sticking around after the night is over. Never let a baller start you out in Doggie-style or any other super-freaky positions. This is a clue that he has you in a fuck-only category. Of course, as a part of sexin' a baller out of his mind you may do the freaky positions, but be sure that a significant portion of the sex was in making-love positions.

How To Ask For Cash & Other Things

Asking For Cash

You want to begin asking for cash indirectly. Talk about some of your financial constraints to him or in front of him. Don't ask for his help though. Act as though you're trying to figure out how to make ends meet. He'll wanna play the role of Superman by saving the day. Promise that you'll pay him back. Of course, you never will, nor will he want you to. But, a week or two later remind him that when you get your next check you're going to pay him back. This keeps you from appearing like a gold-digger. At that point he'll make it clear that it was a gift and that he won't accept your money.

Asking For Other Things

Just as in asking for cash, use subtleness.

To get rent paid, talk out-loud about needing to move to a nicer area, but you're gonna have to find a roommate so that you can afford it. Soon, he'll have a place rented for you and be paying the rent.

To get a car, call him one day and ask him to pick you up because your car is not working. He'll let you borrow his for a couple of days. Later, tell him the mechanic said it'd cost an extraordinary amount to fix the car that well exceeds it's value. Make sure your body language matches the bewildered state that you'd be in if this were really true.

To get jewelry and vacations, use words like "I wish" a lot. He'll wanna make the "I wishes" come true.

Always say thank you to him genuine-like, as though you don't know how you'll ever repay his generosity.

Diversify Your Baller Portfolio

It's always a good idea to keep several different types of ballers in your portfolio.

First of all, the money is great when you have more ballers. Never think that because you are runnin' game on one baller that it'll last a long time. When it sours and the money's gone, you'll be wishing you had more ballers. Secondly, having ballers in different categories reduces the risk of running into another baller you're fuckin'. That shit would be fucked-up! You could lose two ballers on one day!

BIO Of A Baller

Ballers come in all shapes and sizes. Though the following charts are not from an exact science survey, the results are what I've typically found to be true.

Baller BIOs		
Subject	Baller-Type / Rankings	Comments
Most Money	1. Entertainment/Athlete (tie) 2. Heir or Inheritance 3. Real Estate 4. Investment 5. Business Owner 6. Lotto 7. Corporate Executive 8. Street	Entertainers and Athletes tend to have the most money while they're active in their careers. However, their lavish spending habits can make them paupers later. Catch them early!
Biggest Dicks	1. Athlete 2. Street 3. Heir or Inheritance 4. Business Owner 5. Entertainment 6. Real Estate 7. Corporate Executive 8. Investment 9. Lotto	Athlete Ballers are the winners in this category – no surprise. Their large physiques do translate between their legs as well. Street Ballers are a very close second. Heir or Inheritance Ballers spend money on increasing themselves to a nice size too!
Married	1. Corporate Executive 2. Investment 3. Business Owner 4. Real Estate 5. Lotto 6. Heir of Inheritance 7. Entertainment 8. Athlete 9. Street	Stability is desired at many major corporations and marriage is an indication of that to them. If the employee is married, has a mortgage and children's schooling concerns, a company believes he's less-likely to arbitrarily leave the company. This is why Corporate Executive Ballers top this list.
Generous Spender	1. Lotto 2. Heir or Inheritance 3. Entertainment 4. Athlete 5. Street 6. Corporate Executive 7. Real Estate 8. Business Owner 9. Investment	Lotto Ballers are rare, but they spend like crazy from the moment they touch their money! Heir or Inheritance Ballers aren't really being frivolous, they just have it like that and money means little to them because they didn't earn it in the first place. Entertainers like to keep the party going and often foot the bill to do so.

Baller BIOs

Subject	Baller-Type / Rankings	Comments
Fastest Cummers	1. Heir or Inheritance 2. Corporate Executive 3. Lotto 4. Business Owner 5. Real Estate 6. Investment 7. Street 8. Entertainment 9. Athlete	Heir or Inheritance Ballers may have made alterations for size sake, but they can do nothing with endurance, especially when they're not used to wild sex. The same is true with the Corporate Executive Baller.
Desires Anal-Sex	1. Entertainment 2. Athlete 3. Lotto 4. Street 5. Corporate Executive 6. Heir of Inheritance 7. Investment 8. Business Owner 9. Real Estate	The Top-4 ballers on this list are just prone to be wild and more adventuresome. Though this list ranks them by most-common, the bottom-listed ballers are closer to the top than you might think on this subject.
Prefers Large Butt Women	1. Street/Athlete (tie) 2. Entertainment 3. Lotto 4. Investment 5. Real Estate 6. Business Owner 7. Heir or Inheritance 8. Corporate Executive	Ghetto-bootys are valued by all on this list, with the possible exception of the Corporate Executive who might wonder how you're gonna fit that Gansta-booty into a formal evening gown.
Prefers Light-Skinned Or White Women	1. Heir of Inheritance 2. Corporate Executive 3. Entertainment 4. Lotto 5. Real Estate 6. Investment 7. Business Owner 8. Athlete 9. Street	Heir or Inheritance Ballers want a touch of ethnicity, so they prefer light-skinned or multi-racial women that may be closer to mainstream white women. Corporate Executive Ballers feel that lighter skin complexion will make it easier for their date to fit in at company events.

The Right Way To Sex A Baller

Tools Of The Trade

In order to be a successful baller-catcher you must be prepared and have the right tools for the job. Everyone would expect a carpenter to have a hammer.

Your Tool Box Should Include: Push-up bras, thongs, sex toys, condoms, flavored lubricants, lotions, oils, sexy lingerie, etc.

Clothing/Apparel: Diversifying your wardrobe will make your efforts more successful. Because you can't predict what event you may become aware of or invited to at the last minute, having ample supply of different styles of clothing will ensure that you'll be dressed appropriately for any kind of baller that you plan to catch.

Everything you own must be form-flattering or shape-boasting, even the more classy items. Here are some items you must have: Skirt-splits showing off your legs not to mention short-skirts period; Low-cut tops giving a peak at your soft bosom; Tops that stop short of your naval, showing off your tender tummy; See-through shear tops and teasing backless tops/dresses.

Under Garments: Though the baller can't see these items when they first meet you, they are important, especially your push-up bra. A baller-catcher without an array of push-up bras is like a carpenter without a hammer. Though a baller's main focus is still the butt. Recent trends have changed a bit. Ballers are beginning to fall more and more in love with nice titties. So, get the most out of yours, regardless of your cup size by always wearing a push-up bra. I know, they're expensive, but well worth the cost. Stop by Victoria's Secrets to get the very best. Some push-up bras squeeze you together to create cleavage for an open shirt, while others lift your tits higher-up to decrease the distance from your chin to your chest. This look gives you a young-girl appearance.

Also, while you're there find some nice bra-n-panty sets. Vary your selections from lacy to silky. Ballers like variety. Looking at the same underwear, even though it's a different color, is still boring to the baller.

Sex Toys Every Baller-Catcher Needs

There are all kinds of sex toys on the market. Visit any local sex novelty store and ask about them and what they do. If you're hesitant about going inside because you may run into someone you know, I only have one thing to say, "Get Over It!". This is not 1950! And, if you run into someone you know, guess what, they're inside too! Right?

Now, minimally you'll definitely need a *Pocket-Rocket* dildo, which is a smaller vibrating dildo used to massage your clit, as well as insertion. Also, a large-size non-vibrating dildo that'll help *you prepare for the monster-dick ballers. And last but not least, a Butt-Plug* dildo used to become accustomed to anal insertions. I'd also recommend getting a medium-sized vibrating dildo that can be used in your pussy and your ass.

Practice Makes Perfect

Believe it or not, you must practice your sex. Real ballers have had plenty and will be mentally comparing you to all in their pasts. You don't want to be 2nd-Place! You want to be the best they've ever had. To make sure that you achieve this, you've gotta be prepared mentally and physically. Your Sex-Game has gotta be tight! You gotta know what to do, when to do it and most importantly be willing, without hesitation, to do it.

What I suggest is that you attract a man, not a baller, to practice on. In boxing, they call 'em sparring partners. Keep him around long enough for you to get damn good. You don't want to trial-and-error on a real baller, because if you make mistakes, you may have missed a golden opportunity.

Every aspect of sex, you must be prepared for. You can't have a weak-link in the chain. That'd be like a basketball player that practices only shooting, but not passing, dribbling, rebounding and defense. I promise you, if you ain't prepared it will show-up on game day.

As I've said all along, this game is not for the squeamish. If you can't handle the idea of anal sex, girl-girl sex, double penetration, dildos & sex-toys, then you ain't a baller-catcher in the first place. But keep in mind, I ain't sayin' that you're gonna have to do all or any of that type of sex. All I'm sayin' is you're gonna have to be prepared, because there may come a time when all that stands between you and several hundreds of thousands dollars is being able to handle a dick in your ass for 5 or 6 minutes. You've gotta make up your own mind, but I'd be the first to yell, "Lube My Ass Up Good!".

Practice Tip#1: Masturbation

Everyone has masturbated before, but it's different doing it in front of someone else and for the purpose of controlling their mind. For ballers, witnessing you masturbating for them is a *Catch-22*. They love seeing you do it, at the same time it makes them feel insecure because they see that you don't need them to get-off. And, they're wondering if they'll be able to create the same sensation as you've done for yourself. This is a good thing! It gives you subtle power in the bedroom. Use it!

Get together with your sparring-partner. Take your clothes off, SLOWLY, without allowing him to touch you. Tease the hell out of him. Look him straight in the eye as you lick your fingers and use the moisture on them to make your nipples hard. Pinch your nipples and run your hands up and down your entire body. He'll be hard as a rock immediately, but still refuse his repeated attempts to join in. Simply hum sweetly, "Just a minute baby, I want you to watch first."

Also practice masturbation alone to get yourself more accustomed to stimulation, that way it will be tougher for a baller to satisfy you in bed.

Ballers are notorious for going *Clit-Happy*. They love stroking the clit, trying to make you lose control. If you have a very sensitive clit, this could be a problem. Therefore, regular masturbation practice is mandatory for you.

To practice you'll need a vibrator, some KY-jelly and a stopwatch. Turn the vibrator on low and rub it all around your clit until you cum. Remember, only your clit, do not insert it. Check the stopwatch to see how long it took before you had an orgasm. Your goal is to lengthen the time it takes. You must be committed. Repeat this process every night until you can go at least 15-minutes, with the vibrator set on the highest setting, without cumming.

Practice Tip#2: Dick-Sucking Like A Champ

Sucking dick correctly is an art. It's much more than just having a penis in your mouth. To give maximum pleasure, everything must be well choreographed. For a man, dick-sucking satisfies his caveman instincts for superiority, because it is a submissive posture.

Here's a technique that works very well:

First, while standing and kissing him, rub your hands across the front of his pants until you feel him getting stiff. Before he makes a move, you start unbuckling his belt as you slowly glide down to your knees in front of him. Rub your hand against the bulge in his underwear, as you glance up at him. Then slide his underwear off. Grab his dick firmly at its base like its too big for your hand to fit around. Look up at him once again. Use your left hand to hold the base of his dick, as you slowly *jack-him-off* with your right hand. After a few strokes with your hand, lick in a circular motion around the head of his dick. Tease him for about 6-8 seconds before taking him in your mouth. Gradually increase depth in your mouth. Take your time. As your mouth ventures further down his shaft, stroke up and down with the hand that's holding the base of his dick. Move that hand up and down until it bumps into your lips. Vary your speed of sucking from slow to medium, or medium to fast, but never from slow to fast. That's too big of jump and he'll lose the sensation you were building. Occasionally, pull your mouth off completely and let the coolness of the air on his moistened dick make him even harder. Periodically, lick the underbelly of his dick with your tongue or suck on his balls. Take them completely in your mouth, if you can, while continuously *jacking-him-off* with your hand.

How long he'll be able to last before cumming will vary greatly. However, the best way to know when you've got him near an orgasm is not by his moans, but by the size of the head on his dick. Pay attention to its size when you start, use both your eyes and how it feels in your hand. When you feel the head balloon a bit, do not let the opportunity go by to make him cum without giving him a piece of pussy.

Best 2-Ways To Make Him Cum:

The Two-Handed Approach: Wrap left hand around the top of his dick and slide it down to the base. As you do this, attempt to pull the skin tight to the base. With your right hand stroke only the head of his dick. Not long strokes, short ones that focus on the ridge of the head. Use your thumb to rub the underbelly of the head, but don't loosen your grip. Begin at a moderate speed and gradually speed up. Remember to focus only on the ridge of the head! Finally, repeatedly ask him to cum for you as you stroke the hell out of him. If done properly, from start to finish, your hands should be milky in about 90 seconds.

The Freeze-Pop Approach: Just like above, use your left hand to pull the skin tight to the base of his shaft. Barely cover the head of his dick with your mouth. Inside of your mouth, swirl your tongue around the head of his dick. Glide your tongue from side-to-side along the underbelly of the head. With your right hand stroke up and down on the middle section of his shaft, with more pressure being used as you're stroking upward toward your mouth, just the way you'd do when you're trying to push the icy-treat in a freeze-pop to the top. If you're able to deep-throat, do it occasionally. You may even open your mouth with your tongue sliding back-n-forth on the underbelly of the head as though you're ready for his tasty treat. This is the most-effective and fastest cum-producing technique. If done properly it should take no more than 60 seconds to produce his orgasm. Don't be surprised if its 30 seconds or less!

In both the *Two-Handed Approach* and the *Freeze-Pop Approach*, make sure to ask him to cum for you. (i.e. *"Cum for me baby!", "Are you goin' cum for me baby" or "I want you to cum for me baby"*). He already wants to cum and may be trying to fight it because he thinks it's too early for him to cum. Repeat the statements in sync with your stroking.

What To Do With His Cum???:

That's the age old question that always feels awkward to even the most veteran sexual women. Most women focus on getting the *nut*, but never think about what to do with it until that moment arrives. Some suck it in and swallow. Some play with it with their tongue.

Some women let it cover their face like a night-time facial mask. And some rub it up and down his shaft.

The answer of what to do with it depends on what type of baller that you have. You'll have to play it by ear. My suggestion is this: For a Street, Entertainment or Athlete Ballers, swallow. They're freaky like that anyway. They love you 'cuz you're down like that. For Corp, Investment or Real Estate Ballers, rub his cum up and down his shaft. Though they're curious to see if you'll swallow, in the back of their minds they're actually hoping for more sophistication. For Lotto or Inheritance Ballers, use it like a facial mask. These ballers will imagine that they gave you a facial like their favorite porn movie stars. And for the Business Owner Baller, use your tongue to play with his cum. The die-hard romantic will enjoy the semi-ness of the wild-side.

Practice Tip#3: Girl-Girl Sex

This is difficult to practice. First you have to find someone discreet to do it with. The best and most likely candidates are other baller-catchers like yourself. Or a long-time, very close girlfriend.

If you're wondering why it's necessary at all? – It isn't, if you're not planning to ever go after the Entertainment or Athlete Ballers. However, if you are planning to go after them, you'd be surprised what happens at private parties. And before you make the knee-jerk reaction "yuk" face, let's keep it real. I personally don't know a single woman that has not thought about being with another woman at least once. It doesn't make you gay. Women are the sexiest gender to both men and women. It's a curiosity no more taboo than anal, oral or being with two-guys fantasies.

If you have a friend who's a strip-club dancer, you may be in luck. A lot of dancers spend all of their work day looking at other beautiful naked female bodies. They've more than likely had the curiosity satisfied. They could make for excellent teachers.

Whether it's a strip-club dancer you've known or recently met, or a long-time friend, there's still the dilemma of how to get things started. Drinks always help reduce inhibitions or worries about rejections. Invite whomever you choose over to your house. Dress sexy. No matter the gender, sex appeal is important. Spend some time just talking and bonding together. A few more drinks. Move the conversation to the subject of how guys don't know how to satisfy a woman. A few more drinks. Talk about the bad kissers you've dated. Confide that you've always wondered would women kiss you better than a man? Or that you've been curious about kissing another woman, but wanted to do it with someone who wouldn't take your business into the street. This will make her feel comfortable because she knows discretion is important to you.

After the first kiss, I guarantee it will be on! Your body will be amazed by the natural instincts of another woman ravishing you. The more gentle and effective style will surprise you. Breast gripping will feel intriguing because her hands are smaller. The entire experience will be very enjoyable. Make sure to explore all that you want to do, as there's no telling whether or not she'll be willing to do it again without the *spur-of-the-moment* liquor slumber party that you created.

Practice Tip#4: Anal Aerobics

Anal sex is one of the toughest hurdles for a baller-catcher to overcome. Thoughts of pain and feelings of degradation prevent many women from exploring this area. It's a mistake. Your willingness to allow anal sex, when done at the right moment after setting-up the baller, can result in him giving you money at a rate you've never imagined, or even a marriage proposal (where you can later take half of his millions)! So, get over it!

Start by using lubrication lotion or oil. Gently rub a well-lubed finger back and forth across the hole. Do not plunge your finger in right a way. Instead, increase depth gradually, adding more lubricant if needed. Soon you'll be able to take in a full finger. Try rubbing your clit at the same time as you're fucking your ass for added stimulation. Some women even climax from anal sex.

To prepare your ass for anal sex with a dick, you'll have to do it in phases. Once you've mastered pumping to a full finger, you'll be able to move on to using a narrow dildo that's wider in circumference than your finger, graduating to a normal dick-sized dildo. You want to make sure that you're able to handle anal before you allow a horny-ass baller get in you. Never allow a huge or mega-size dick anywhere near your ass. Besides the pain it may cause, it can stretch the muscles and make every baller that fucks you later think that you're just a ho when they see the new size of your asshole.

Practice Tip#5: Double Penetration

Double Penetration or "DP" is normally done in doggie-style sex when a baller inserts a finger into your ass. This is especially stimulating for him as he can feel himself through the wall that separates your ass and pussy. DP is also done with two men as you straddle one facing him and the other man inserts his dick into your ass. You'll have to be a real ruff-ryder to handle this maneuver. To practice, insert a dildo in your pussy, at the same time, use your finger or tiny/narrow dildo to insert in your ass. Be sure to prepare your ass by using lots of lubricating oil.

Sex Tips & Techniques

It is important that you remember that sex with a baller is not for enjoyment or physical gratification – it's about the money!

Gain Control Of Your Body - Sexually!

In this high-stakes game of Baller-Catching, I can't stress enough how important it is to gain control of your body, sexually. Failure to do so will have catastrophic results. Sexual-inferiority will make it virtually impossible to keep a baller around long enough to run your game.

The whole purpose of using the *Practice Tips* is so that your body becomes well-versed. The more you practice, the harder the baller has to work to satisfy you. Thus giving you the sexual advantage over him. That's the name of the game!

Ballers tend to have big-egos when it comes to sex. Some may be entertainers bragging about their sexual prowess in music videos. If you're able to wear-his-ass-out in a short period of time during sex, you've gained control over him. He doesn't want others to know that. Plus, he feels it inside no matter what.

To achieve this, you must know your own weakness. Don't lie to yourself. Work on whatever are your weaknesses until you've overcome them. If you can't handle thick dicks, get a dildo that size and keep practicing fucking yourself until you ain't shivering and cumming in the first 20 seconds. If it two-fingers in your pussy that drives you wild, get your sparring-partner to put three-fingers in you until it's no big deal anymore. If there's a certain sex-position that you lose all control of your body while doing, that's what you work on, over-and-over again!

A Ballers Most Sensitive Sex-Spots!

Knowledge of a ballers most-sensitive sex spots is key to turning him out in bed. Men have many areas that drive them crazy that women have ignored.

Ears – A swirling tongue inside the ear or gentle biting of the earlobe can be enough to make a baller's dick rock-hard instantaneously!

Butt – With the exception of ball players receiving the pat on the backside after a good play, men rarely feel direct contact in that area. Squeezing the but during sex is a incredible stimulant to men. Maybe even a full body massage that focuses on the butt area. Believe it or not, some straight-men (not gay men) actually don't mind the massaging, even slight penetration directly in the anus. With him lying on his back, rub oil all over his genitals, suck on his balls as you jack his dick with one hand. Then, with the other hand, sneak an oiled finger down the crack of his butt and slowly slide it up and down the seam until you work your finger to the hole. Use gentle pressure. If he's not pulling your hand away, then he must want it, so stick it in the hole. You'll find out how exhilarating it is to be on the other side – you're actually fucking him!

Nipples – A man's nipples can be just as sensitive or more so than women's. Biting, pinching and squeezing turns him on, too. Be gentle, though. His nipples are smaller than yours and an over abundance of pressure can be painful to him.

Balls – Try this out! With him lying on his back, lift his dick out of your way as you circle your fingers around where the base of his dick meets his balls. Put his entire balls sack in your mouth and suck hard with pressure. Continue this pressure as you pull your head back until his balls pop out of your mouth. You should hear a popping sound. A sure-fire way to hear him begging and pleading with you!

Feet – Massaging the bottom of his feet will drive him wild! So will sucking on his toes, one at a time!

The Rules Of Engagement

Force In-Town Ballers Make A Date With You

Always make ballers that reside in the same city as you (In-Town Ballers) to make a date with you. You don't want to give them the upper-hand by allowing them to use you as a one-night stand. That would only make your job more difficult when you try to run your game on them because they'll already view you as an "Alternate" because you were too damn easy!

Obviously the rules are slightly different when it comes to *Out-Of-Town* ballers like rappers or athletes who may only be in your city for one-night, at most a few days. In this case, it's most important to make the connection. But in doing so, still attempt to keep some control when you hook-up with them, later that night. You set the time and get a cell phone number under the pretense that you'll call them later. Trust me, they'll be back in-town on another tour-stop or to visit you. After you've done your thing with them and they've left town, if you're planning to contact them using the cell phone number, you may want to do it quickly as these types of ballers tend to change cell phone numbers like they do underwear. That number may be good for only a couple of months.

Never Let A Baller Eat Your Pussy!

Despite what you've seen in the *Top-20 Sex Positions Ballers Love* and even though it's a difficult to resist the temptation of having a luscious, willing tongue flicking back-n-forth across your clit sending shivers through your entire body, you must remain strong and never allow a baller to eat your pussy. For most women, oral sex creates uncontrollable stimulation and orgasms. Allowing a baller to witness your ass *orgasmically* flapping around on the bed like a fish out of water, creates a feeling of accomplishment. To him, he'll be thinking, *"Okay, I knocked her off, it's time to move on"*. I'm giving you fair warning right now. Regardless to how many men you've had eatin' your pussy and you were able to control your body's gyrations, you have not had real oral until you experience it from a baller. They are simply the best! So, do not take on ballers on their home-field because they are World-Class Pussy Eaters that will have your eyes permanently stuck in the back of your head and your legs still shaking 2-hours after he's left your house – they're that damn good! You've been warned!

Now, with that said, there's only one exception to the rule. Oral is acceptable only with Business Owner Ballers (*BOBs*). It is because they are die-hard romantics that it doesn't disadvantage you when they get your ass cumming like a water-sprinkler. It actually endears them to you because they're already insecure about their sexual ability. They'll feel like they've found someone that they can greatly affect and will somewhat become addicted to your orgasms.

Only For You, Baby!

When it comes to sex, never act as though you've done anything often before. I don't care what it is. It's always your first time and only for him. When sucking his dick, act apprehensive at the mere idea. Start off awkwardly as though you don't really know how to do it, before turning into a dick-sucking champion. Ballers are stupid enough to think that somewhere in the middle you magically figured out how to do it well. Or that you got so excited about his dick that you just had to suck it ferociously. They want to believe that they're training you. If it's anal sex, act as though it hurts a bit. He'll be dying to try to go deeper and will be more than gentle, hoping to allow you to get adjusted to his dick in your ass, so that you'll let him continue.

Keep Your Pussy Tight!

I'm not just talking about grooming. Yes, shave the pubic hair or trim it down, at least. Ain't nothing more nasty to a baller than a woman with wild-ass pussy hairs. Bald pussy ballers love as well! Along with grooming the outside, you gotta take care of you kitty inside. Douche regularly!

Also, ballers hate it when a baller-catcher's pussy is worn-out. They can't even get a good feeling of friction because the pussy is that loose. If you've had children or just a lot of sex, it's only natural that your pussy can become loose. But that still don't help you catch a baller.

To help tighten the pussy muscles, I suggest using *Ben-Wa Balls*. They are metal balls that are inserted in your pussy and you must use your pussy muscles to keep them from falling out. Using these regularly will help you to be able to clamp your pussy around a baller's dick so tight you'll have his ass screaming like a school-girl! Another way to regain that tight pussy like a virgin is to use products called *Vaginal Tightening Cream.*

Undressing is Revealing, not Stripping!

This may seem stupid and unimportant, but it isn't. When you're taking off your clothes to have sex, do it slowly. It's a teasing factor that stimulates his brain. Don't rip-off clothes. Glide them off like a ballerina. Even show concern for them, as you take time to fold them and place them neatly on a dresser. Occasionally, glance at him as you're removing an item, catch him salivating and trying to fix his face to a cool-demeanor, while you charmingly smile back at him.

Top-20 Sex-Positions
Ballers Love!

#1 Regular Doggie-Style

The most classic of the baller sex-positions. Ballers love the ass and this position allows them to see yours waving and shaking. Plus, they're able to penetrate deeper. This is the #1 position that a baller is normally in when he cums.

#2 Standing Doggie

Ballers love this position almost as much as Regular Doggie-style because he's able to use his legs to thrust, while using his arms to forcefully to pull you back onto him. Powerful slapping strokes and the mere sound of your butt making a clapping sound as your flesh meets his is an exhilarating aphrodisiac.

#3 Sling-Shot Doggie

The *Sling-Shot* position is another booty sound-effect making maneuver that is a favorite of the baller. The restraining of your arms satisfies his caveman instincts for feelings of power and control.

This move is not for everyone. Be careful of extremely well-endowed ballers – you may not want them to have this much control!

#4 Horses Reign

Similar to the *Sling-Shot*, the *Horses Reign* feeds the natural male ego with a sense of dominance. By tugging on your hair, the baller feels again, in control.

Hair pulling should not be of a rough-nature. Gentle tugs or the constant tension on the reign of hair is the point of this position. Be prepared for ass-spanking by his free hand, as he'll most-likely be unable to resist wanting to be a jockey.

#5 Regular 69

Always perform *69* with you on top. This gives you the ability to do a better job than the baller. Constantly move your hips around in random directions, thereby making it difficult for the baller to catch your rhythm and out-perform you in *69*.

As I mentioned earlier, I do not suggest that you give the opportunity to a baller to perform oral-sex on you. However, this is one of their favorite positions. Should you choose to engage in this maneuver, just make sure you can out-perform him!

#6 Standing 69

Mostly Athlete Ballers perform this maneuver because of their superior upper-body strength. They have to be strong enough to hold you. Be careful not to create too much stimulation for him while you're in this precarious position. You do not want him to lose his grip on you.

#7 Leap-Frog

Leap Frog will test your arm strength, as the man is on his toes with his weight leaning forward onto your shoulders that are being support by your arms. Though very similar to *Doggie-style*, you'll be surprised by how much the stimulation is increased by the slight difference in angle of entry!

#8 Gateway Arch

His tongue in your *Gateway*, creates the *Arch* in your back. Making this position the *Gateway Arch*. Nuff-said!

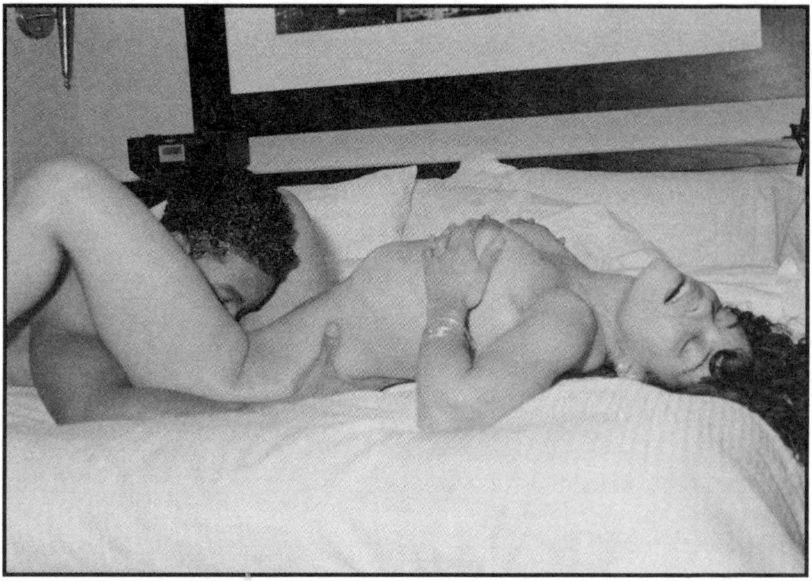

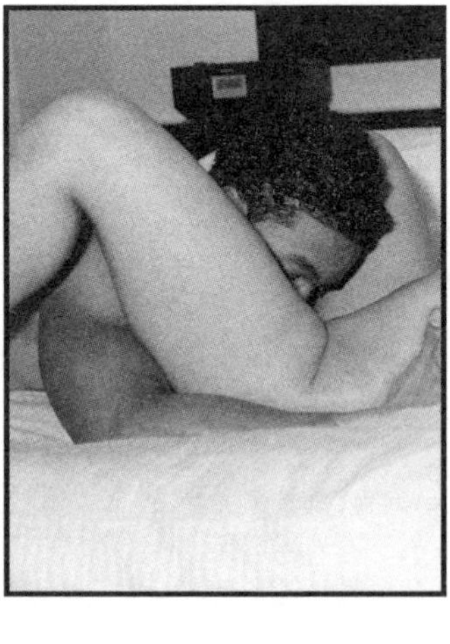

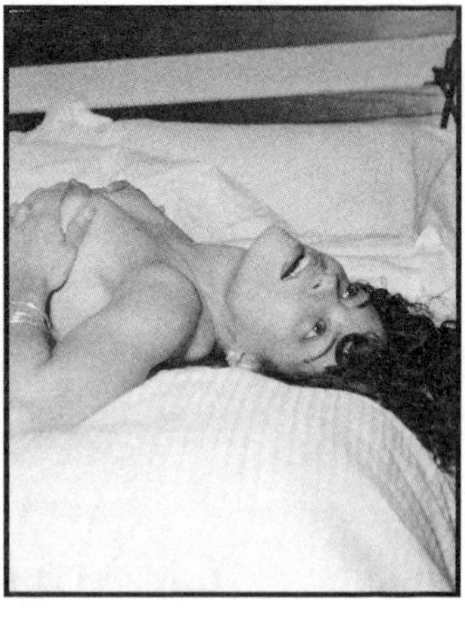

#9 Double Chair

The *Double Chair* is a position of the more gentle and more romantic ballers. Partner-facing positioning is conducive to love conversation sensual bonding that's based less on stroke-intensity and more on intimate sensitivity.

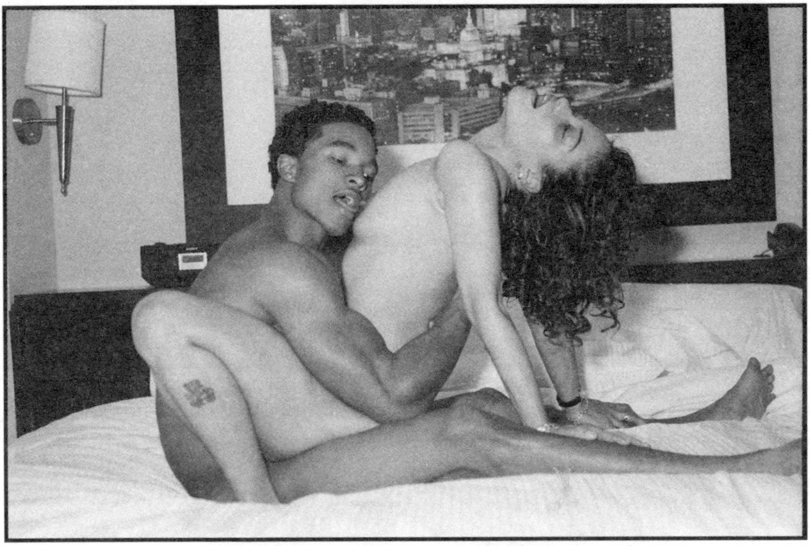

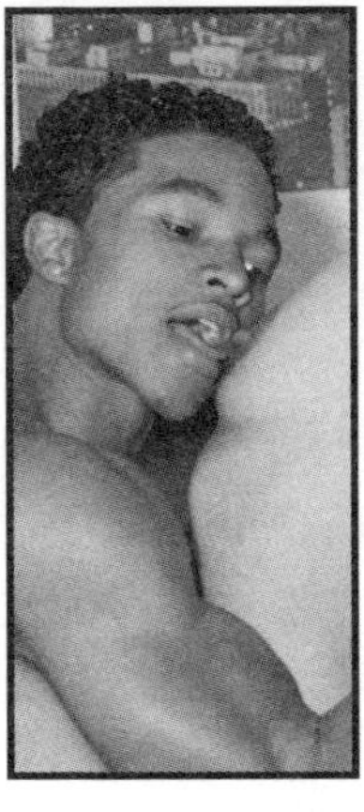

#10 Cow-Girl

Ride 'em Cow-Girl! Nuff-said!

#11 Reverse Cow-Girl

Work those hips, gurll! Nuff-said!

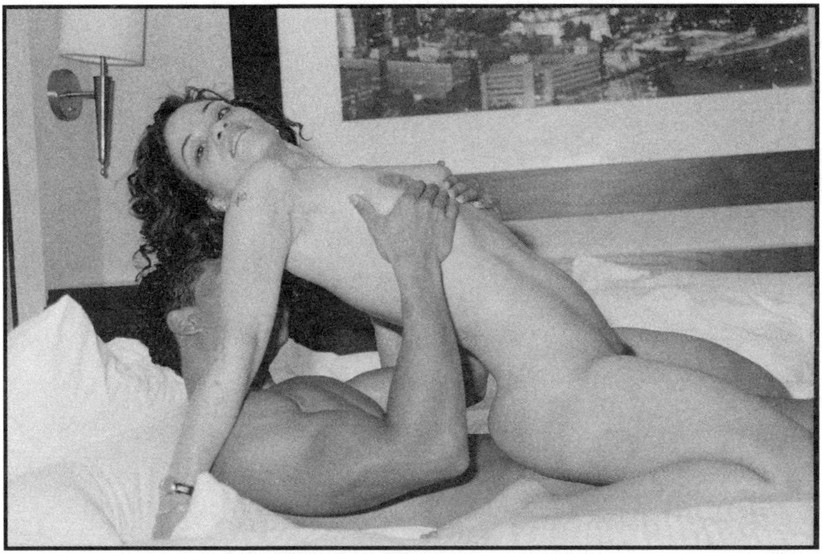

#12 Missionary

The *Missionary* position is used primarily by the more sensitive ballers. However, some of the other ballers may use it as a starting point of sex. But, you can be sure they will not stay in this position long, as they'll be anxious to get you into the more exotic positions.

The *Missionary's* face-to-face contact conjures thoughts of wedding-bells and creates an intimacy-level that the baller may not be comfortable with for an extended period of time.

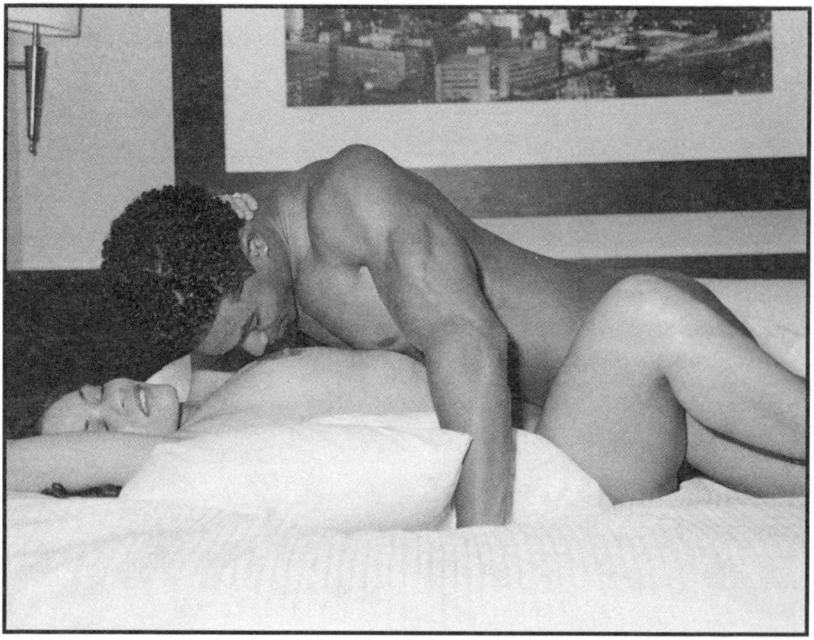

In most cases, you will not have to request a change in position – he'll do it for you. But if he doesn't, you may want to take charge.

#13 The Bridge

The *Bridge* is a very sensual position for you and the baller. Using his muscular arms, he pulls you back and forth up to him. He's no longer pumping, as you've become the stroke.

He may use one hand to gently support your lower-back as his other is free to glide a thumb across your special spot.

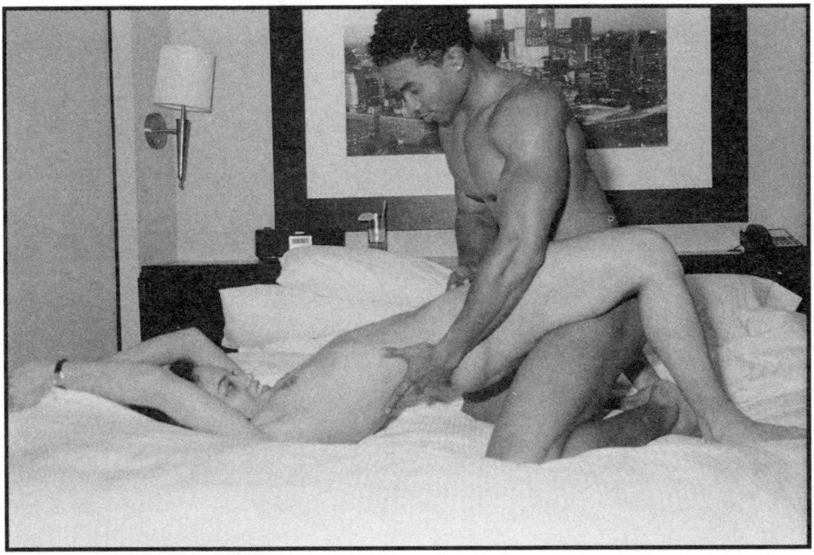

Be careful not to lose your damn mind in this position, it's very easy to do.

This position should come with a warning-sign. **WARNING: Multiple-Orgasms Ahead – So, Slow Your Ass Down!**

#14 Sex Carry

Ummph! That's all I got to say!

#15 Face Mask

Day-ayy-ummm!

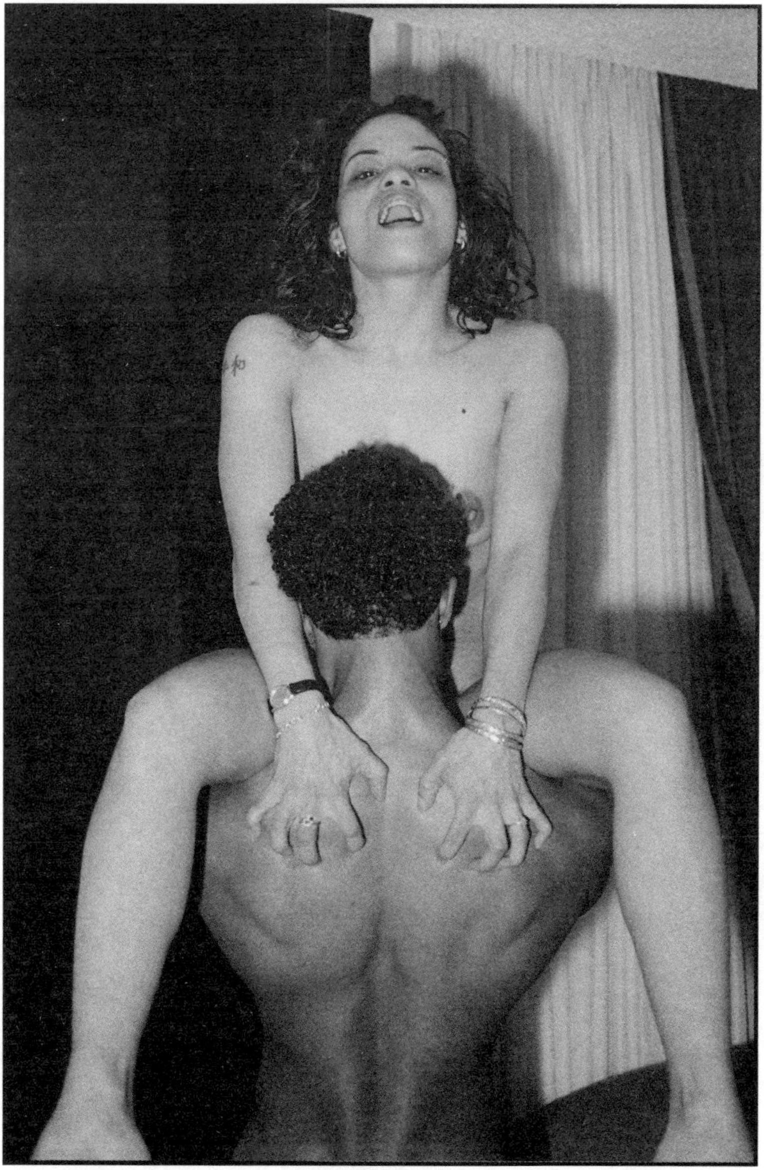

#16 Two-Hand Jack

Learn it! Do it well!

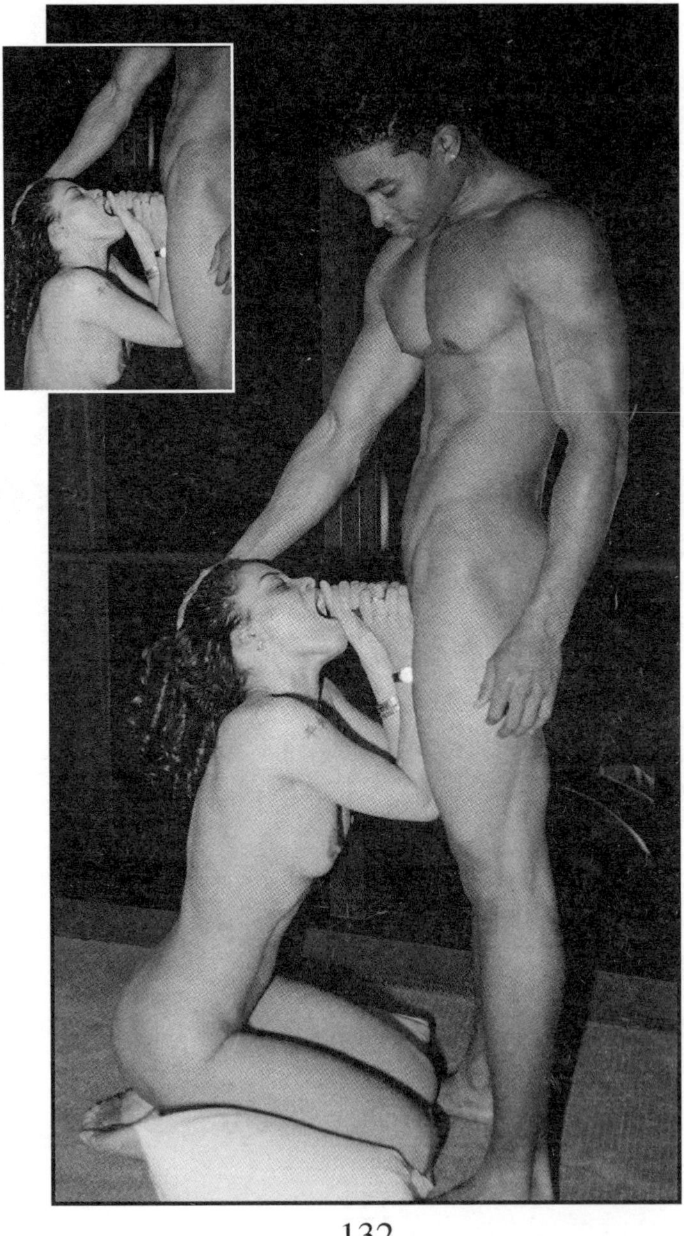

#17 V-Formation

Ballers love the access they get in the V-Formation!

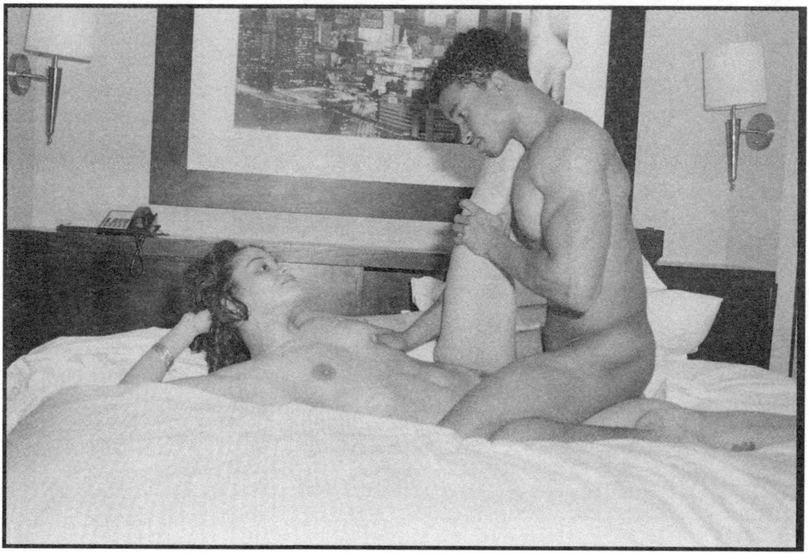

#18 One Leg Raise

Done in *Missionary-style*, the *One-Leg Raise* allows a baller to get more stimulation by enabling him to reach more depth. It's a more intimate position because you're face-to-face.

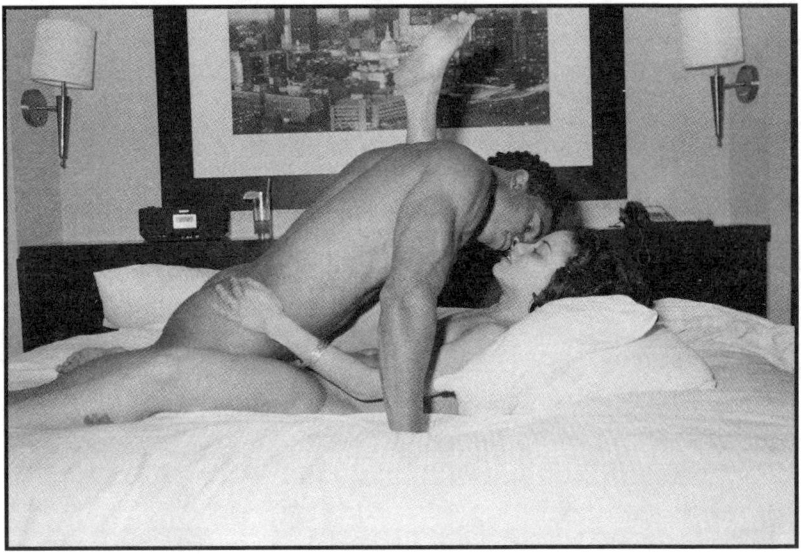

Be sure that you can handle his pace in this position because it is very-likely that he's going to really put it on you!

Your safety-valves in this positions are your hands. Use them to push on his stomach to limit depth, if needed. You can also use your hands to grip his butt to slow him a bit. Your hands gripping his sensitive butt will create a stimulation in him of possible pre-mature ecstasy that he'll want to avoid by slowing his stroking.

#19 Free Throw

This maneuver is called a free-throw because with both of your legs being controlled by his hands, he's free to throw it on you with deep rapid strokes.

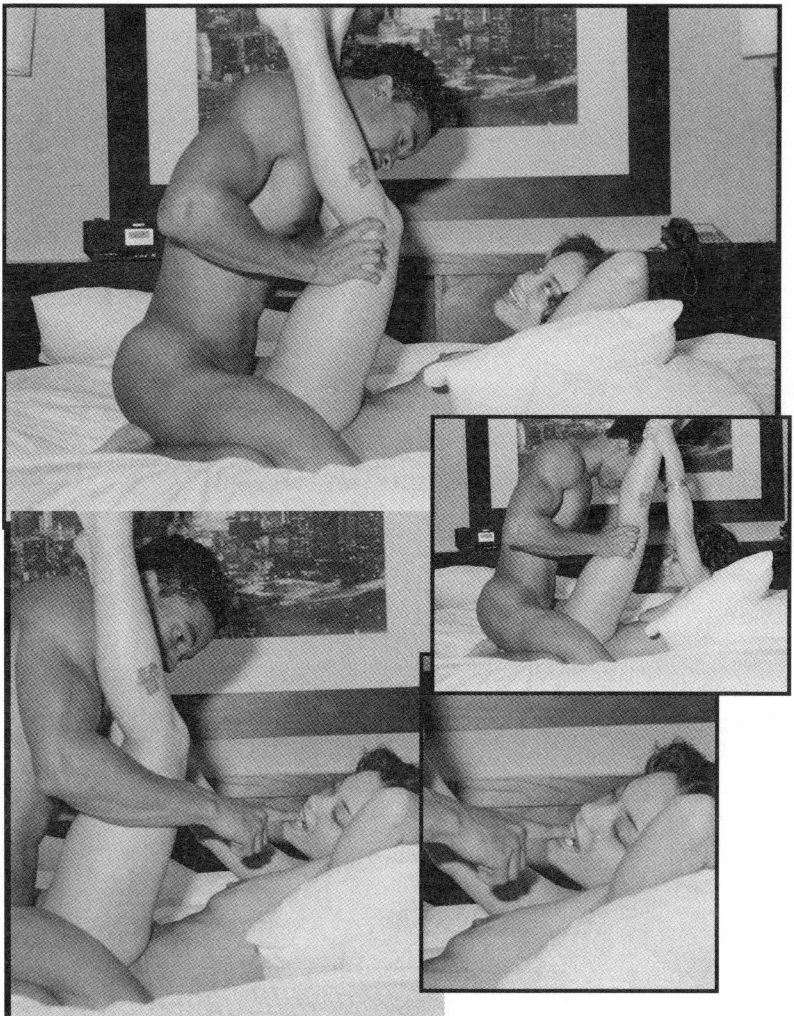

#20 The Grind

The Grind is a sensual exploration of every crevasse of the body with hands. Usually done as foreplay or even post-play.

Gettin' Dat Cash!

Baller-Catcher Success Stories

"Limo For Love"

Baller-Catcher: Chantè
Age: 21
City: (Undisclosed To Protect The *Not-So* Innocent)

I've been a huge fan of my local NFL team for years and had a special thing for one of it's defensive players that I thought was sexy as hell. I wanted to meet him somehow, but the odds were very good that that wouldn't happen unless I did something drastic.

During the beginning of the season, I rented a limo and was driven to the practice facility around the time practice had ended. I rolled down the tinted glass and told everyone of the staff that walked by to tell the player I wanted badly that his limo was waiting for him.

I couldn't believe it when he emerged from the building. He was even sexier in person. He walked towards the limo with a confused look on his face. As he got close to the limo, I lowered the tinted window to reveal a sexy-dressed me in the back seat.

"Are you the one that said that there was a limo for me?", the handsome player asked.

"Umm-hmm", I chirped back at him.

"I'm sorry, there must be some mistake. I didn't order a limo.", he replied.

"No there's no mistake.", I said, opening my blouse flashing him a quick view at my braless breasts. "Hop in!", I continued waving him in.

He looked around to see if anyone else had seen my flash before opening the door himself and climbing inside.

"You're something else!", he said with a boyish grin and a shake of his head.

"Oh, you don't know the half of it. But you will by the end of this ride", I said as I gave instructions to the driver to begin driving.

Without so much as giving him my name first, I kneeled between his legs and pulled out his long dick. I licked all around it before placing in my mouth and bobbing my head up and down.

Attempted several times to deep-throat it all, but it was just too damn long.

When he finally pulled me off of him, I knew that I was about to get the fuck of my life 'cause his dick was by far the largest I'd seen. And I was right.

At first, it felt as though he was stuffing a cucumber into a pencil sharpener. But soon my muscles relaxed and I was riding that dick like I was a championship bull-rider at a rodeo as he was double penetrating me with his finger in my ass. I'm tellin' you, if I had a nickel for every time I screamed *"Oh shit!"*, by the end of that limo ride I'da been as rich as him.

One hour and 11-orgasms later, well 12-orgasms if you count his, we arrived back at the deserted sports training facility parking lot, so that he could drive home in his own car.

One week later, he'd kick his fiancé to the curb that he'd dated since high school, driving up to my apartment in a limo bearing an $8,000 diamond tennis bracelet for me and asked if I wanted to take another ride. – you know I did!

"Music Lover"

Baller-Catcher: Bianca
Age: 24
City: Harlem, NYC

One Saturday morning, I was listening to Hot-97 on the radio and heard that one of my favorite romantic R&B performers was gonna be promoting his new CD at a music retailer on 125th street in Harlem.

I was so glad that I'd gone to the salon the night before because I wouldn't have gone to the event otherwise. I rushed in and out of the shower and hurried to 125th street.

When I got there, the line was already ridiculously long and it was cold & windy outside. I was a die-hard fan, so that wasn't gonna stop me. There was absolutely no place to park and I wasn't gonna miss my opportunity to meet my favorite star. So I took my chances by double-parking and got in line.

It took almost 45-minutes waiting in line before I was near the front door. Just as I made it to the front door the security guard informed everyone that was behind me that they were cutting the line off because the star had other engagements. The people in the crowd were pissed off. They started yelling and screaming. I could understand them because I probably would've been one of them had I not been the last person they allowed in the door.

A small disturbance started breaking out, as security decided to close and lock the front door of the music store for the protection of the star.

Inside the door, there was still quite a line in front of me. I kept an eye on my double-parked car as I moved forward in line while witnessing security attempting to calm the fans that were denied entrance. Soon, the police were called-in to de-escalate the situation. Just as I was making it to the front of the line, I witnessed a white and blue police tow truck towing my double-parked car away.

"Damn it!", I said out loud.

"Hey sister. Calm down.", I heard a voice say.

As I turned around, it was my favorite R&B singer, speaking to me. I'd been so busy checking the status of my car that I'd not been aware how close to the front of the line I'd gotten. It wasn't the way I'd envisioned meeting him, with the first words out of my mouth being curse words.

"I'm sorry. They just towed my car away.", I said to him, frustrated in my predicament.

"Don't worry love, I can get you a ride home.", he smiled, as he looked around for one of his people to inform of my situation.

It was then that I'd noticed that most of the people left in the store were either employees of the store or record label personnel. The fans that were in front of me had been ushered out of the back door due to the disturbance.

"No that's alright. I can call a friend.", I said handing him his CD to sign.

"What's your name, love?", he said.

I was flattered that he asked until I realized that is was so that he could write it on the CD that he was signing.

"Bianca", I said, leaning over the table to watch what he wrote.

"Bianca, that's a pretty name!"

"Thank you."

"Bianca fits you perfectly. A pretty name for a pretty lady with a pretty smile.", he charmed me.

My smile was wider than a kid's on Christmas morning.

"You should give me your number, Bianca, maybe we can hook-up some time?", he said intrigued.

I gave him my cell phone number, because I wanted him to be able to reach me whenever he called.

"Now you ain't giving me a fake number, are you?", he played with me, knowing damn well that that wasn't the case.

As I left the store walking home to call one of my friends to ask for a ride to the police impound lot, my cell phone rang. The display on my phone said "private caller".

It was him.

"I hope I'm not calling you too soon!", he giggled.

"You are crazy!", I blushed back.

"I was just wondering if you wanted to go get something to eat?", he offered.

"When? Right now?", I was surprised.

"Yeah, right now. Unless you've got some man that you have to get back too.", he taunted me.

"I ain't got no man.", I clarified.

"Well then, why don't you turn around and come get in the car. I'm in the black Navigator behind you.", he said as he honked the horn.

Inside I was thinking, *Damn! He was following me. I've got a music-star-stalker.* Then I started thinking about how I was walking and every move that I made while I was unaware that he was watching me.

I climbed in the car and we drove down 9-A to Lower-Manhattan to a small, chic Italian restaurant that he enjoyed.

The whole time I was trippin' about how down-to-earth he was. And about how he asked me out just like any regular guy would've done.

After lunch, he drove me to the impound lot and paid for the ticket and impound fee to get my car released.

I'd declined his offer to pay originally, until he said that he'd be offended if I didn't take it. I told him thanks and gave him a peck on the cheek.

I thought I'd never see or hear from him again, but he called me later that night.

"There's something about you that's just cool, ya know?", he spoke genuinely to me on the phone. "I'on't know what it is, but you just kinda cool like dat".

That night, I met him at his hotel, *The Plaza* on Fifth Av.

We sat around like old buddies, ordering pizza and in-room movies. We even laughed and joked as we watched music videos and mockingly danced doing imitations of some of the stars, like he wasn't one of them.

Around 1:30 in the morning, I caught myself yawning and decided that I better go.

"You don't have to go. I mean, you can stay here. I'll sleep on the sofa or I'll rent you a room. I'm just enjoying your company.", he said, convincing me to stay.

"You don't have to rent another room. And you don't have to sleep on the sofa.", I returned with smoldering eyes.

The whole day had turned into one big date that led to this moment.

He sang one of his songs, as he slowly walked over to me, wrapped his arms around me and gave me my own personal concert.

We made real love that night. Slow, passionate, heart-touching, soul-stirring sex.

For the past six months later, I've found myself a permanent resident in his sunny Los Angeles mansion, spending his money on fine clothes, jewelry and driving a convertible Benz!

We've even talked about getting married. I'll make sure we do that in California, so that when I divorce him a little over a year from the wedding, I'll be entitled to HALF!

What's his name? That's for you to guess!

"Fill'er Up!"

Baller-Catcher: Angela
Age: 29
City: Atlanta

I'd been a customer of my local gas station for years. I knew everyone that worked there and they'd address me by my name as I'd pay for my morning coffee and doughnut.

Another common face to me was a guy that I assumed was a manager or a regional manager for that chain of gas stations. He was always dressed professionally in a shirt and tie and seemed to be doing inventory, as he'd carry around a clipboard. And whenever he was there, I could tell a difference in how the employees would act.

I never got to know his name because I'd only see him every so often, as he was there about once or twice a week. But, because I was there every morning, his face had grown familiar. I'd thought about asking his name, but was never curious enough to remember to do so after I'd paid for my coffee.

It wasn't until one of the female employees, Gladys, told me that he was asking about me after I left on the previous day, that I became interested in who he was. It was more from a precautionary stand point.

When she explained that he wasn't a manager or a regional manager, but the owner of this and six more gas stations, I began getting very interested.

I already thought that the very-fit early-40's man was handsome, but wasn't my type. After the news of his gas station empire, I decided right then that he was my type – rich!

I hinted to the cashier that I'd noticed him too and left. I knew she'd not be able to resist playing match-maker, especially when her boss had confided his interest in me to her. It'd make it easier for him to approach me by having secret information that I might be interested.

Sure enough, the following morning the owner was there. For him, being there two days in a row was unusual. So, I knew he was there for me.

As I walked up to the counter with my normal cup of coffee and doughnut in hand, I'd noticed that he'd strategically come from behind the counter as I approached.

When I attempted to pay for my items, he waved the transaction away by using hand-signals to Gladys.

"Your coffee and doughnut is on me.", he said in a smooth voice.

"Oh, well thank you!", I acted surprised and smiled back at him, while purposely delaying putting my wallet back in my purse so that he'd have more time.

"I see that you come in here alot!", he attempted to strike a conversation, unsure of how much time I had to chat.

"Yep, every single day.", I informed him of my loyalty.

"My name is James Martin, I'm the owner.", he said without being boastful, yet he made sure to get it in.

"Nice to meet you James. I'm Angela.", I responded without giving my last name.

"Listen, Angela....", he began speaking with a more serious face, as he guided me away from the counter, mindful of both the customers and Gladys' ears. ".....I know you don't know me, but I was wondering if I could take you to dinner sometime?", he finished, clearly nervous about my answer.

I blushingly smiled, "Yeah. That sounds very nice, James."

We exchanged phone numbers before I got back in my car and imagined that James was getting a high-five from Gladys.

After that day, I never paid for another tank of gas again. I'd even forgotten how expensive it was to fill-up the tank of my SUV.

I'd purposely moved-in with him for six-months before breaking off the relationship.

Under Georgia law, if a man and a woman live together for more than six months they're considered to be common-law spouses. Each person is entitled to half of what the other has. I sued James taking full advantage of this law and accepted a hefty 6-figure settlement along with large-sum alimony payments, as opposed to actually going to court where I could've gotten more, but I might've also had the case thrown-out.

Now, I no longer have to work.

CONGRATULATIONS!!

By completing this book, it's my proud pleasure to bestow upon you the Certified Baller-Catcher's Degree! This degree is like no other. You've earned it! Now, go make me proud!

Baller-Catcher University

Established, since the beginning of time.

This certifies that

____

has satisfied all requirements, is a member in good standing and is hereby granted all the rights and privileges pertaining thereto. This **Certified Baller-Catcher's Degree** allows it's recipient to use it to get cash, jewelry, cars and other living expenses paid for by any and all unsuspecting ballers that are too stupid enough to know that they're being played.

____

Date

Mysterious Luva

Mysterious Luva, Professor & Dean
Baller-Catcher University